Old Light

Old Light

© 2020 by J.S. Watts
ISBN: 978-1-946050-20-5

Strange Fictions Press
An imprint of Vagabondage Press LLC
PO Box 3563
Apollo Beach, Florida 33572
http://www.vagabondagepress.com

First edition printed in the United States of America and the United Kingdom, February 2020

10 9 8 7 6 5 4 3 2 1

Old Light

J.S. Watts

Strange Fictions Press

CHAPTER 1

He was, to a casual observer, a small unexceptional man, precisely dressed in a well-pressed grey suit, a crisp white shirt, and a plain, to the point of boring, dark blue tie. Except boring was too positive an adjective for the overall effect. Also, the crispness of the shirt was being seriously threatened by the rivulets of sweat currently pouring down his face and neck and, increasingly, his upper torso. This profuse sweating was unpleasant for a wide range of fairly obvious reasons. It was also remarkably surprising in an experienced, 100-year-old witch. Not that he looked like a centenarian practitioner — more like a forty-year-old auditor who was badly out of his depth.

The cause of his embarrassing perspiration problem was sitting directly opposite him, at home in her own comfortably, but expensively, antique furnished lounge. If you didn't know her, you would have said she was in her late twenties, but whilst her mid-brown hair was immaculately bobbed, and her face and figure were attractive, she wasn't generating the sort of sexual allure that makes grown men break out in a hot, salty sweat. She was wearing a classically plain and shapelessly rather prim, beige, cashmere dress and balancing a delicate, porcelain teacup and saucer on her right palm.

Slightly repositioning her five-foot, 100-pound frame in the eighteenth-century, leather fireside chair she was sitting in, Holly Beldam continued to stare far from casually at her troubled visitor.

"And why, exactly, Brother James, would I want to do that?"

"It's really quite an honour, Sister Beldam. Very few are invited to assist the Coven in its endeavours, and of those who are, even fewer are ladies, let alone ladies who have come into their powers quite so late in mundane life as your good self."

"But, then again, mine are extremely strong powers for a lady... or a man, come to that."

"Indeed, they are, Sister Beldam, and with them you could help the Coven mightily."

"As I said, before, Brother James, why, exactly, would I want to do that?"

Brother William James felt another wave of tell-tale sweat soak into his once pristine and now decidedly soggy shirt. Holly was still staring at him, and now she wasn't blinking. William was reminded of a hungry and rather irritable bird of prey that was considering whether the object in its line of sight was edible. He broke her gaze by glancing down towards his feet, only to find a pair of bright green eyes looking up at him. They weren't blinking either. Their owner, a sleek black and white short-haired cat, was studying him the way it would a fascinatingly plump rodent. William wondered whether wearing the mouse-grey suit had been such a good idea. He looked back up at Holly. Her wide, hazel eyes were still fixed on him, and she was waiting.

He automatically attempted to loosen his now rather constricting shirt collar with a damp index finger, as yet more sweat trickled down his neck.

"I've mentioned the honour, right? The very *high* honour, given your gender." Holly nodded slowly, without breaking eye contact. It was not an encouraging nod. "The abnormal strength of your witchlight could really help to make a difference. So many possibilities. Plus, your working closely with us could help us understand Old Magic that much better. There are so few practitioners left."

"And why do you think that is, Brother James?"

There was a brief, uncomfortable pause.

"It's okay. I'm not expecting you to tell me. Indeed, I'm going to tell you." Holly pointed a finger sporting an ornate moonstone ring directly at Brother James.

"For generations, your coven has chosen to persecute those of us who are able to harness natural magic: pursued, persecuted, and killed. Yes, one of my family has, until very recently, been stupid and misguided enough to kill our own in the name of preserving the magic, but that is now history. The Coven has been doing what it does for far, far longer. And what does it do, by the way? When I was trying to stay alive long enough to save me and mine and put an end to the killing, what did the Coven do? Nothing. Abso-bloody-lutely nothing. I can only assume that, a little under a year ago, they would have been more than happy to see me die. Yet, here you are, on their behalf, asking me to help them. Let me tell you, Brother James, I am willing to help them by just as much as they helped me. Tell them that, will you?"

The hazel eyes blinked, and William James suddenly felt as if he had been released from invisible, but very strong, bonds. He was up and out of his seat almost instantly. He even managed not to look back to check for sweat marks on the chair's upholstery.

"Oh dear, Brother James, off already? I was about to do my duties as a little lady hostess and offer you another cup of tea."

"Err, no, thank you. But no, I really couldn't presume. I have taken up so much of your time already. And your hospitality. I really should be going."

As he propelled himself towards the lounge door, he almost trod on the black and white cat. He staggered but thrust a rather clammy hand forward and braced himself against the nearest wall. A pair of aggrieved green eyes shot him a look of reproach and were suddenly joined by a pair of saffron yellow ones, as a large marmalade cat emerged from under Holly's chair and, hissing, blocked his line of escape.

"Grindlebones," admonished Holly.

The ginger cat walked slowly, and rather reluctantly, back towards her.

"Is that Partridge Mayflower's familiar?" William surprised himself by asking.

"No, he's one of mine, but Partridge was his witch before being incinerated alive trying to give me the help the Coven didn't — wouldn't — offer me. I took Grindlebones in and looked after him. He adopted me. Did you know cats have surprisingly long memories?

Very sensitive animals, cats." A pause. "If you like, Grindlebones can escort you to the front door?"

"No, I'm fine. Really. I can find my own way out." *Not nearly quickly enough,* said a voice in his head. He wasn't sure if it was his subconscious or a woman's sarcastic voice he was hearing, but he didn't stop to ponder the matter.

Opening the lounge door, he walked as quickly as he could, without running, along the plain, white-walled hallway. It was a relatively short walk, but he could have sworn the hallway was longer than it had been when he had entered the cottage. It certainly felt as if it was.

Before he had reached the end of the hall, the heavy wooden front door swung open of its own accord and, as soon as he had exited through it, swung-to again behind him. It closed with a resounding thud, but Brother William James, Senior Witchfinder to The Grand Coven of Great Britain, Ireland, and the Etheric Isles in their Domain, did not hear it. He had already disappeared in an implosion of pale grey light.

***

Inside her old and rather picturesque black and white cottage, Holly was making a big, loving fuss of her two cats.

"Well, do you think that'll get my message back to the Coven, boys? They've been persistent. I'll give them that. What do you think they'll come up with next?"

Outside, in the lane at the front of the cottage, a big, grey rabbit suddenly appeared, ran across the road towards the black and white timbered cottage, and scurried into the base of the thick hawthorn hedge surrounding the property's unseasonably colourful front garden. There, it sat and cleaned its large and alert ears, while keeping its darkly watchful gaze focussed on the cottage.

CHAPTER 2

Dusk was surreptitiously rising up from the Oxfordshire countryside around the cottage. The two cats, Barny and Grindlebones, wandered out to confront it and claim as much of its territory as possible for their own. At the same time, they intended to see whether there were any small, helpless rodents worth terrorizing prior to consuming them for supper. They strolled purposefully out of the back door, leaving Holly alone and wondering what to do with herself.

She put down the book she had been flicking through. The cottage had a lot of books thanks to Holly's grandmother, Ninanna Beldam, who had both built it and begun a personal library within it back in the seventeenth century. She had unintentionally left the cottage and its contents to Holly upon her sudden, unexpected demise during a fatal confrontation with Holly, which she herself had initiated.

Since then, Holly had had eleven months in which to read and absorb much of the book collection. Fascinating stuff, but none of it really got to the heart of living with the family-size portion of Old Magic she had also inherited from her late and unlamented grandmother. It was all about getting the power and keeping the power, not about how you coped with the power once it was yours for keeps. More importantly, none of the books offered any insight as to how a newly powerful witch might lead a fulfilling and nearly normal life in the twenty-first century.

"So what shall I do now?"

Not surprisingly, the cottage didn't answer. Something else attempted to, though. In Holly's head, at the back of her skull, and just behind her right ear, there was a faint dry rustling. It had been there, on and off, ever since the confrontation with her grandmother. Holly shook her head and ignored it as she had been doing for the last eleven months. Over time, it was becoming easier to ignore.

Holly pottered around for a bit and then decided it was time to go home. Not that she wasn't home already, but her partner, Jake, would soon be at their home — her other home — and she liked the idea of being at that home to meet him when he got back from work. That necessitated her leaving home to go home.

Things would have been easier if Jake had been willing to live in the cottage in rural Oxfordshire, but his veterinary practice was near Cambridge and, if truth be told, he was uncomfortable about living in a place so full of magic. So, the domestic, relatively mundane home remained in a village in South Cambridgeshire, and Holly routinely commuted between the two properties.

Sealing up the Oxfordshire cottage for the night, Holly walked out of the back door, down the cottage's rear garden path, through the orchard that lay beyond it, and from there walked across the nettle and thistle filled field at the back of number sixty-six Basingfield Lane, over the back fence, through the well-kept winter garden, and in through the back door of number sixty-six. Home again. Seventy-odd miles in well under two minutes. Literally a home from home.

In the Cambridgeshire house, Holly spent all of three minutes cleaning the house from top to bottom and adding a sprinkling of witchlight to make it seem that much more welcoming. Then she prepared supper. That took another minute. She didn't want to rush things. Jake liked well-prepared food.

Now what could she do? It wasn't even quarter to six yet, and Jake probably wouldn't be home before six-thirty at the earliest. The two cats weren't likely to come in for hours, and all the books she was reading were back in Oxfordshire. Of course, she could always magic a book or two over, but for Jake's sake, she chose not to. This was, of course, really stupid, because she used magic in the house for domestic purposes. But, if it kept him happy…

Holly picked up the phone and dialled her friend Sarah's number, but she wasn't home. All Holly got was:

"Hi, this is Sarah and Mike's phone. If you're calling for Mike, leave a brief message and your phone number. If you're calling for Sarah, tell me all your news and gossip and take as long as you like. Either way, one of us will call you back as soon as we can."

Holly left her message:

"Hi, Sarah, it's Holly. Give me a call when you've got a moment. I'm... well, I'm a bit bored, actually, and I could do with a chat. Maybe we can meet up for lunch this week. But a chat before then would be good too. So, call me, please."

Now what?

There was that question again.

Holly found herself asking it more and more often these days. A flood of magical power running through her, almost limitless possibilities at her fingertips, and she didn't know what to do with herself. How pathetic was that?

She picked up the phone again.

"You've reached the answer phone of Jake Wortham. Please leave your name and number, and I'll get back to you as soon as possible."

"Hi, love, it's me. Just wondered what time you're going to be home tonight. Give me a call, yeah? Love you."

So again: now what?

She could always take herself off for a bit of impromptu sightseeing; fill in the hour or so visiting the Uffizi or the Hermitage. She could do anything she wanted to, anywhere in the world (except bring about world peace – some things were just too messy and complicated even for feral magic), but that assumed she knew what it was she wanted to do. The rustling behind her right ear grew momentarily louder, but Holly blocked it out once more.

She turned on the state-of-the-art television in the lounge and flicked through all the standard channels and then some less standard channels using her witchlight. She finally came across a re-run of a Seventies U.S. show she hadn't seen for decades and settled down to watch that. She was still watching it when Jake came in. He hadn't bothered to return her call and arrived home unannounced.

"Hiya, Prickles. I'm back. It's been a long old day. I'm just going to grab a shower, and then we can eat, yeah?" He went straight upstairs before Holly could answer. Holly sat and listened to the sound of the shower running upstairs with a sense of resigned inevitability that hadn't been there six months previously.

While Jake was sorting himself out, Holly focussed her gaze on the dining room table and watched while it laid itself. The parade of crockery, glassware, and cutlery used to amuse her with its echoes of children's cartoons, but these days it was just part of the daily routine. She magicked up a vase full of fresh, unseasonal flowers for the centre of the table and a bottle of extremely expensive Merlot. Then, once again, she stood wondering what to do with herself. Upstairs, the shower was still running.

She wandered, rather aimlessly, into the utility room. The two cats' bowls, one functional brown and the other a slightly lurid bright green, were already piled high with cat food — for the look of it, more than anything else. Cats are always conscious they have standards to maintain. If the boys came back after a successful evening's hunt, they wouldn't want more than a mouthful of biscuits each, but Holly understood that the possibility of more was important.

Jake finally finished showering. He came downstairs looking tired but refreshed, his black, but lightly white-flecked hair still damp and sticking to his scalp. Under the old navy blue sweatpants and T-shirt he was wearing, his lean and well-muscled frame looked appetising. Holly walked towards him to give him a passionate hug but was greeted with an absent-minded peck on the cheek.

"What's for dinner, Prickles?"

Holly magicked their perfectly cooked and steaming hot dinner onto the table: stewed steak and dumplings, boiled potatoes with mint, carrots and peas. When it came to food, Jake was a traditionalist. Meat, potatoes, and two veg suited him just fine. The smell of the food wafted upwards with the steam. Jake smiled and then sat down to eat without saying a word. Six mouthfuls in, he managed, "This is nice."

Holly looked up hopefully, "Do you like it?"

"Mmmm. I just said so, didn't I? All your cooking is top notch, these days. The joy of magic, I guess."

"It doesn't hurt the process, but you have to know what you're doing to begin with." Holly breathed out audibly. "How was your day?"

"Bloody knackering. The Clopside Estate cows needed a thorough going over, and it's a large herd. Plus, it was raining for most of the time."

"Poor you."

"Yes, well I haven't got your wonderfully convenient witchy powers to make my work easy and keep the rain off."

"I could always help you, if you wanted. There's plenty of books on animal husbandry in Ninanna's collection, and with your expertise, I probably wouldn't need them much anyway."

"Yes, Prickles. Thank you, but I'm a vet. I use science, painstaking study, and years of hands-on experience to treat animals in need of my care and attention. I'm not keen on any unnatural short cuts."

Holly felt the need to defend her position. "Witchlight is totally natural. It's both a genetic ability and a practical tool. The outcome of using it is as real and natural as the effects of a dose of bovine antibiotics or whatever."

"Maybe, but I'm not a witch. I'm just a bloody good vet."

"I wasn't suggesting you weren't."

Jake shovelled more of his dinner into his mouth and said nothing.

"If you're that tired, how about a short break?" Holly suggested. "Somewhere hot and sunny where you can put your feet up for a bit."

"I can't afford to take any more time away from work. We've been away six times since the end of my sick leave. How many holidays do you want to take, for heaven's sake?"

"Just a weekend, maybe?"

"Look, I'm well. In fact, I'm fully recovered and better than ever, thanks to your magical interventions, no doubt. I don't need any more rest, and I'm quite happy to spend time at home when I'm not working."

It was Holly's turn to focus on her food, but she didn't like the resultant silence.

"I had another visit from the Coven, today, someone called Brother William James. Apparently, he's their Senior Witchfinder."

"They already know you're a witch and a very powerful one, at that. What do they need to send a witchfinder for?"

"It's not what he does that's significant. It's the level of his rank that matters. Each time they send someone, they send someone higher up the food chain." Jake carried on eating. Holly tried again. "They are really trying very hard to win me over."

"So, why don't you go work for them?"

"What? After they pointedly declined to lift a finger to help me when Ninanna went on the rampage? Partridge was the only one who was willing to cover my back, and he died trying to help me. If they'd helped, maybe he wouldn't be dead. How can I forgive that? Plus, if Brother James and his predecessors are anything to go by, they are a drab collection of antiquated, petty-minded, misogynists. It's a big no thanks to any job they might be thinking of giving me."

"Well, there you are, then. Just tell them to stop sending people round." Jake shovelled the last forkful of the main course into his mouth. "What's for pudding?"

Holly clapped her hands, and the empty dinner plates disappeared. Another clap, and two generous helpings of homemade — or at least home-magicked — apple pie appeared in their stead.

"Custard, cream, or ice cream?"

The mumbled response wasn't totally clear, but the comforting smell of warm custard soon filled the dining room. Jake seemed happy with the outcome.

Several forkfuls into dessert, and something sounding like the onset of World War Three broke out in the utility room: yowling, miaowing, squeaking, and scrabbling, accompanied by varied loud thuds and crashes. Both Jake and Holly got up in a rush to investigate, but Holly beat Jake there. He had to run, and she just transported herself with a subtle puff of shimmering white air. Even so, she arrived too late to do anything other than survey the carnage.

In the middle of the floor, a bloody patch of tiling was surrounded by strewn flesh and fur. There was also a small steaming pile of unpleasantly wobbly purple entrails. Two cats with blood-stained mouths and cheeks sat on either side of the chaos, each with a sizeable chunk of what had once been a large, grey rabbit in his mouth. Other recognisable bunny body parts were scattered more widely, including the remains of a head with remarkably large ears and a pair of swiftly dulling black eyes. Holly thought she fleetingly sensed a fading waft of witchlight, but there was no obvious sign of magical involvement, just a very dead rabbit and two contented, if somewhat bloody, cats, proud of having done what cats naturally do.

CHAPTER 3

Holly and Sarah had arranged to meet up for lunch at a small café in town they both liked and that had been close to both their places of work, back when Holly had had a paid job. These days, it was still convenient for Sarah.

A chilled bottle of Chablis sat on the table between them. Sarah was helping herself to another glass, despite saying earlier that she wouldn't be having too much because she had an afternoon meeting to go to. The act of pouring the wine didn't inhibit her contribution to the flow of conversation,

"I really can't see why you're bored. Since you came into your inheritance, your not-unsizeable inheritance I should say, you've been constantly on the go: sorting out the cottage, going on holiday with Jake, doing up your own place, going on holiday with Jake again (and again) and — though I know you deny it — I suspect there's been a bit of nip and tuck going on. You're definitely looking younger than your thirty-nine years and don't forget you're turning forty this summer.

"I can't see that you've got the time to be bored, and if you are, well, you could always go shopping or take yet another holiday. Why not start arranging the big birthday bash I'm sure you are thinking of holding for all of your deserving friends? Given those possibilities I wouldn't mind being bored. Anyway, if you are bored it's your own fault. You chose to give up your job. You could have carried on or gone part time or something. You could always do some voluntary work, you know. Mind you, I'd welcome the chance to chuck it all in, abandon all my case files, and spend the days shopping and socialising." Sarah paused at last to take a sip of her wine.

"Yes, I know I'm damn lucky, and it was my choice to give up work. At the time, it seemed to make sense. But now life has settled down a bit, I'm finding I've more time on my hands than I thought. I've worked full time, solidly, for almost twenty years, and the change is taking some getting used to."

"Well, all I can say is that if I had your money I wouldn't be complaining of boredom. I wish. Go shopping, take up a ridiculously expensive hobby. Here, what happened to those Chinese lessons you were having with that cute tutor? God, he had a good arse. Pheasant somebody?"

"Partridge. Partridge Mayflower." Holly kept a firm grip on her emotions, which were suddenly trying to knit themselves unpleasantly in complicated patterns. "Partridge isn't my tutor anymore."

"Had a little tiff, did we?"

"No. It wasn't like that. He... erm... had to go away. Anyway, we'd done as much as we could together."

"So, learn another language. Find another cute instructor. If you don't tell Jake, I'm sure he won't mind." Sarah winked.

"I'm not sure he'd mind even if I said I was having lessons with George Clooney."

Sarah paused in the act of moving a forkful of linguine towards her mouth,

"Are things all right between the two of you?"

The delay to Holly's response belied the affirmative, "Yes."

"So, what's up?"

"I said yes."

"Yes, you said yes, but you communicated no. Plus, it wasn't that long ago that you and he were both talking wedding bells. But nothing's happened, and I haven't heard the slightest mention of a ding-dong in weeks. How are you and Jake?"

Holly fiddled uncomfortably with her chicken salad.

"There's nothing wrong, as such."

"But...?"

"But...vwe don't seem to spend much quality time together these days. Perhaps we over did the time together when I... came into the money and Jake was recuperating. We did take a lot of holidays, but now Jake seems wholly married to his work and is not at all keen if I even suggest a weekend break away together."

"He's probably just grateful to be fit and well and back at work after that awful dog attack. He's a member of the weaker sex, remember, so he probably thinks he's got something to prove in terms of a return to full strength."

"You're right. He is behaving as if he's got something to prove. I keep telling him he hasn't, but I don't think he's listening."

"How does he feel about your inheritance?"

"Sorry?"

"Well, maybe there's more than one reason he feels he's got something to prove. Presumably you paid for all the holidays and stuff? Was he okay with that, or did he feel beholden? Men don't like that, you know. Remember Spencer? He never forgave you for bailing him out — literally, I might add. Does Jake feel he owes you, has become dependent on you, or at least your money? Now me, I wouldn't be unhappy if you wanted to go away somewhere sunny and exotic and felt like taking me along for the ride, all expenses paid." Sarah grinned in exaggerated hopefulness. Holly laughed, and the mood at the table lightened a little. "So where is it we're going?"

Sarah eventually went back to work to tell everyone the exciting news of her soon-to-be trip to the Maldives, whilst Holly sorted out the arrangements for the holiday on route back to the Oxfordshire cottage.

Holly materialised in the cottage's back garden and had only just let herself into the flag-stoned kitchen via the back door when she heard a resounding knock at the front one. Surprised, she went to open it. An unknown man stood there wearing a visually uninspiring grey suit and a plain dark tie. She was reminded of Brother James from the Coven, and it came as no surprise when he said,

"Sister Holly Beldam? I'm Brother Marcus Wainthorpe. I'm a Coven Inquisitor. I was hoping I'd find you in. I'm trying to track down Brother William James. Do you mind if I come in?"

"Err, feel free."

There was a sudden pop of rapidly expanding air as a second male witch, dressed in the uniform grey suit, materialised directly behind Marcus Wainthorpe.

"Brother Lincoln is with me."

Both men strode in through the front door. Holly's face formed itself into a weak and tight-lipped smile as they brushed past her and as she tried very hard not to take offence at the way they scrutinized the cottage during the short walk down the hall and into the lounge.

When her two visitors were seated, Holly proffered tea and biscuits as usually seemed to be required by Coven officials. She was surprised, but not upset, when both men declined her hospitality,

"No thank you, Sister Beldam. We are keen to hear what you know about Brother James' last movements, and then we will be on our way."

"Last movements? That's sounds bad. How can I help?"

Brother Wainthorpe was apparently the loquacious one. Brother Lincoln limited himself to examining every inch of the lounge that he could see from his seated position. This involved twisting and turning in ways that had to be seriously uncomfortable, if not actually physically impossible.

"We understand that Brother James came to visit you three days ago with a generous invitation to you from the Coven to come and work for us?"

"Yes, he did come to talk to me about a job offer."

"We further understand from his report back, sent in shortly after the meeting, that you surprisingly declined the invitation and apparently in a way that left Brother James feeling highly uncomfortable."

"I declined the offer, yes, but you'll have to ask Brother James himself about whether it made him uncomfortable."

"If only we could, Sister Beldam, if only we could. But, as Brother James disappeared not long after visiting you here, we find ourselves unable to do that otherwise very natural thing."

"Oh dear, I'm sorry to hear that. I do hope it had nothing to do with me unnerving him in some way." Holly felt that the necessary niceties were especially necessary at this moment but was still not quite sure why.

There was a brief pause while Brother Lincoln removed a small, black, leather-bound notebook from his inside jacket pocket, along with a cheap black biro, and pointedly wrote something down. Then he returned to his corkscrew study of the lounge. Marcus Wainthorpe resumed his questioning,

"So, you admit you unnerved him, then?"

Holly didn't like the tone of the question.

"No. I said I hoped it had nothing to do with me unnerving him, because you had implied that he was uncomfortable. There is a difference. A significant difference."

The air in the lounge was becoming chilly, but Wainthorpe didn't appear to notice.

"I see. Did Brother James seem unnerved when he left here?"

"He seemed quite keen to leave."

"Had you done anything to make him eager to go?"

"I offered him a second cup of tea."

Brother Lincoln's notebook came out again, and he made another scribbled note.

"Anything else?"

"Possibly a biscuit. I can't really recall."

"No, I meant did you do anything else to him that might have made him desperate to get away from here?"

"I didn't *do* anything. I did, however, tell him precisely what I thought about the Coven and its less-than-generous offer. He then clearly felt the need to leave. Why, exactly, are you asking me this?"

Marcus Wainthorpe matched Holly stare for stare.

"After his visit to you, Brother James didn't return to the Coven offices as expected. His last reported location was in the lane, just outside this cottage. When, considerably later, we ran a tracer spell to try to locate him, it indicated that he was, erm, mostly present in a field in Cambridgeshire. In a field behind Basingfield Lane, in the village of Basingfield, South Cambridgeshire, to be precise."

"That's where…"

"…You live with your mundane partner, Mr. Jake Wortham. We know, which is why we would like to know what you've done to Brother James."

"I've done nothing to Brother James. Feel free to write that down too," she added, as Brother Lincoln's little black notebook made yet another appearance. "I made every effort to be reasonably polite to the man, despite some of his Neolithic attitudes and the fact he upset my cats. He left the cottage under his own steam and via the front door. I, however, would like to know what he was doing apparently hanging around the back of my home in Cambridgeshire after he left my property here."

Marcus Wainthorpe did not react to Holly's increasing irritation or the now-plummeting temperature in the lounge.

"So would we, Sister Beldam, and we would further like to know what happened to him whilst he was there."

"Happened?"

"The tracer spell was, on this occasion, aptly named. It found traces of him in the field. In different parts of the field. Simultaneously. Whilst we failed to identify any obvious remains, we have had to assume that Brother James is no longer with us, so to speak. No longer with *us*, but he was last known to be here, with you and afterwards, near here, near to you and after that, spread around a field there, near to you. So a connection to you in some form or other seems a reasonable supposition."

Holly really didn't like Brother Wainthorpe, or the direction of his thoughts, but she had to admit that she could see their logic,

"As a supposition, it's not unreasonable, but factually it's incorrect, as far as I am aware. If you are right in inferring that there is a connection between us, perhaps the Coven knows something about it? Is there something you want to tell me, Brother Wainthorpe? Was Brother James spying on me on the Coven's behalf, say?"

Holly and Wainthorpe continued to exchange fixed stares. A third pair of eyes, bright green and with a slit rather than a round pupil, watched this human stand-off with fascination. Barny approved of his witch's appropriate demeanour and was contentedly smug when Brother Wainthorpe was the first to break eye contact. He was also proud that his witch continued to glare at Wainwright even after he had looked away. Very commendable from a feline perspective. If Holly sensed this silent approval, it didn't interfere with her discussions with Marcus Wainthorpe.

"Well, Brother Wainthorpe, I am waiting. I am sorry for Brother James' apparent disappearance and even more sorry if it has been caused by his death, as you imply. God knows, the Coven has been implicated in more than enough deaths already. I, however, am left asking why the Coven keeps sending its representatives to pester me, to make me patronising offers I can and do very easily refuse, and then why one of these representatives disappears in close proximity to my mundane and, as far as I am concerned, very private home. On top of all this, I also want to know why the Coven now feels it is necessary to send two further grey-suited officials to ask me questions and why one of them, when he is not trying to emulate a twisted rubber band, keeps scribbling away like a mute obsessive/compulsive note-taker? Has this intimidatory approach been authorised by the Coven?" Holly broke eye contact with Wainthorpe long enough to glare at the still frantically scribbling Lincoln. The scribbling stopped abruptly. Holly then returned her focus to Wainthorpe. Barny quietly purred his satisfaction with his human's solid stance.

Brother Wainthorpe's stance was finally becoming less solid,

"I assure you, Sister Beldam, the Coven wants to get to the bottom of this as much as you do. The Coven has considerable respect for the power of your witchlight and your command of Old Magic, which is why it continues to hope to work with you, despite your negative responses to date, and why there are two of us asking you questions this afternoon. We are unhappy and perturbed by Brother James' disappearance and simply wish to, um… mitigate any undue risk to Coven representatives who have occasion to visit you in the future, either here or in Cambridgeshire. I am sure you understand."

Holly understood all too well. The air temperature in the lounge dropped several degrees further. Even Barny fluffed up his fur to keep the warmth in. Brother Lincoln breathed heavily on the hand he was not once again writing with. His breath was clearly visible on the cooling air.

Brother Wainthorpe coughed and said, "We'll be leaving you for now. Should you think of anything that might help us in our enquiries in relation to the disappearance of Brother James, please do contact me." He proffered an ordinary, plain looking business card, but Holly sensed the magics surrounding it. It was, literally, a calling card. She took it reluctantly, grudgingly impressed that he had the power to make such a device. Few in the Coven seemed to. Whilst the magic necessary to construct the card was not strictly Old Magic, it came close.

"We'll show ourselves out," Brother Wainthorpe concluded.

The two male witches got up and made their way to the front door. Barny followed along in their wake. If they had had any thoughts about taking a detour on their way out of the cottage, Barny's presence put paid to that, as did the discovery, when they opened the front door, of Grindlebones sitting on the front doorstep. The ginger tom slowly got up, stretched, and vacated the step to permit them to exit. He maintained close scrutiny of them, however, as they walked down the front garden path, and his yellow eyes didn't blink until they had both disappeared in a combined implosion of two tones of grey air.

Job done, both cats meandered off in search of something interesting to eat, ever hopeful of finding a rabbit as large and distinctively flavoured as the one they had dragged into the Cambridgeshire house the other evening. Holly wasn't the only one who could walk between the Oxfordshire and Cambridgeshire properties without breaking stride.

CHAPTER 4

Holly was nerve raspingly angry. She had been seriously irritated by Brothers Wainthorpe and Lincoln while they were sitting in her cottage. Now they had gone, and she'd had a chance to reflect upon their discussions, the irritation had grown and blossomed into something far larger and fiercer. The rustling behind her ear mirrored her anger and performed a crescendo of its own. Despite this, Holly continued, pointedly, to ignore it.

"Bloody, petty-minded bureaucrats. They're quick to point a finger but take no responsibility for their own dubious actions." She stared accusingly at her half-drunk cup of tea sitting innocently on the occasional table in front of her. "How dare he go to Basingfield Lane? What on earth was he doing there?" The tea in the cup was rippling. Then the cup visibly started to vibrate. "Petty-minded, hypocritical, interfering…" The cup rattled violently against its saucer. "Ignorant, ineffectual, petty-minded…" On the repetition of "petty-minded," the delicate porcelain gave up the ghost and cracked into three, spilling its tepid contents into the saucer and over the occasional table. Holly paused in her tirade, mopped up the puddled tea, and pieced the tea cup back together again with a waft of witchlight. At least its temporary destruction had interrupted her rant and made her think a little more calmly.

"Petty-minded fools" had been Ninanna's frequently and loudly stated opinion of the Coven. When had Holly acquired her grandmother's view of things, along with her turn of phrase? And was this an inheritance Holly really wanted? If that wasn't bad enough, what was she doing talking out loud to herself? She was starting to lose it and over a pair of petty minded… That phrase again. Was it really sensible to be so dismissive of the Coven and its members?

Sure, the Coven lackeys who visited her came across as grey-suited nonentities and jobs-worths. Yes, the generations of accumulated witchlight that flowed through her veins made her far more powerful than any other witch she had yet met. But… But there were many witches she hadn't met. If truth be told, she'd kept herself to herself while she had adjusted to the power that had unexpectedly come her way. It was dangerous to underestimate deep-rooted institutions like the Coven. It had survived for centuries, when hundreds and perhaps thousands of allegedly powerful Old Magic practitioners had faded into oblivion or worse. If feral magic was so powerful, why were there so few witches left who used it fully? Admittedly, Ninanna's homicidal accumulation of power was unprecedented in recent centuries and therefore, Holly couldn't really judge the normal strength of Old Magic. But just because she had unusual amounts of power didn't mean she couldn't still be vulnerable. Even one less powerful witch in the right circumstances could undermine her, let alone a coven-full. So what exactly had Brother James being doing at Basingfield Lane? Had he been spying on her and if so, why? What was the Coven up to? Or was Brother James working for himself or someone else?

Holly took a firm grip on herself and applied the brake to her surging emotions. This was stupid. Paranoia wasn't going to help any more than anger.

"I'm just rattled, is all. Their implied accusations were unexpected and upsetting." She stopped. She was talking to herself again. Clearly sedentary introspection was not a good thing at the moment. She decided she needed to do something other than sit around and gnaw away at things she couldn't change.

The thing Holly decided to do was run a tracer spell herself on Brother James. At least that way, she could verify what the Coven officials had told her. Little more than a year ago, her then-mentor Partridge Mayflower had accused her of presumption when she'd offered to run a tracer to look for the allegedly missing Ninanna Beldam. She could hear his voice laying down the law:

"And just why do you think a newly illuminated witch like yourself is going to do better than your elders and Coven members, who have no doubt tried this ad nauseum. What does that say about you, precisely? Any witch who lets her power go to her head is doomed for the darkness, let me tell you, girlie."

But that was then and maybe if she had searched for Ninanna at that time, things would have worked out differently. Maybe Partridge would be here in the flesh to nag her himself. Now, of course, only his memory could reprimand her.

She had much more power now than she had then, plus a nagging dose of trust-no-one. Having your maternal grandmother try to blast you to smithereens, let alone admit to killing both your mothers, your biological father, and your mentor, was more than enough to induce a healthy sense of paranoia. Checking up on Brother James and the story the Coven had told her seemed plain sensible in light of all that.

The search for Brother James was a relatively quick affair; most things involving magic were a relatively quick affair for Holly these days. Despite the simplicity of the act itself, however, acting on the results was not that simple. Brother James appeared to be indirectly present in the field behind Holly's Basingfield house — in several places in the field behind Holly's house. At the same time.

Holly went outside to investigate. As before, it didn't matter that she had started out in Oxfordshire. Within little more than a few steps, she was in the Cambridgeshire field, but there wasn't that much to see. The feral version of the tracer magic she had used led Holly to the most secluded parts of the field, under broad bushes and in the densest of thickets. When she arrived at the indicated spots, there was little there: flattened grass, scuffed undergrowth, bare patches where blood had clearly been spilt. Whether the kill had been made by foxes or cats, Holly couldn't tell, but these were all places Holly's two cats frequented. Cat runs they had made were invariably nearby, as well as physical signs of cat toileting. Holly checked, and the depositors were frequently, but not always, Barny and Grindlebones. The indicated presence of Brother James — even if Holly couldn't see him — was linked to the cats, or at least their habitual locations. Finally, Holly found some torn grey fur and some rabbit bones. The boys or a fox had definitely dined here, or it may just have been the rabbit remains from the previous night's excitement. Holly probed the bones further. Her witchlight told her that they were closely associated with Brother James in some way. Holly was not convinced, but the more she checked, the more it became clear that the tracer magic looking for the Coven acolyte was picking up on rabbit remains, blood and, rather yuckilly, cat shit.

Holly returned to the house — the Cambridgeshire one. Barny and Grindlebones were happily ensconced in the kitchen. Holly stared thoughtfully at them as she recalled in blood-smeared detail the unusually large rabbit they had dragged into the kitchen the other evening. She had carefully had the remains relocated out into the field where anyone or anything could have found them and spread them around still further. Two pairs of eyes stared innocently back, or as innocently as any cat can. She was exceedingly grateful she had made them take the bunny bits outside and had then thoroughly cleaned up the house after them the magical way. But had the field adjacent to the house been such a good idea?

Still, there was nothing more she could do. That was that, then. Bye-bye, Brother James, probably. So, now what? This time she didn't even notice the dry rustling at the back of her skull, so there was no need to ignore it.

So, now what? That question again. It was one she seemed to be asking herself a lot these days. Well nigh limitless magical power, and she still didn't know what to do: with herself in general or now, about Brother James (or what was apparently left of him).

There were still books in Ninanna's cottage that Holly hadn't read. Now seemed like a good time to exhaust their knowledge. Maybe their pages would give her an answer — or at least the sense of direction she seemed to have been lacking for some time. Brothers Wainthorpe and Lincoln and their missing and broadly spread-out colleague were an added incentive.

Up until now, Holly had been reading the books slowly, the old-fashioned way: a page at a time. It had seemed the appropriate thing to

do. It took time, patience, and commitment, but mostly it took time
— used it up, and kept Holly occupied. The alternative, absorbing
the information stored within the books through the direct flow of
her witchlight, brought back memories from the previous year that
Holly wasn't prepared to deal with just yet. Also, Jake had become
strangely reluctant to have her use her power too often, at least in a
way that he noticed. His tacit approval of her mundane, studious
ways had provided further motivation to read through Ninanna's
library the painstaking way.

Now, with the unsettling visit of Brothers Wainthorpe and Lincoln
still fresh in her mind, along with the disturbing, scattered, and
blood-stained locations of Brother James, Holly wondered whether
it was the right time to finish reading her grandmother's book
collection the fast and effective way: by witchlight. Notwithstanding
the still rather sensitive memories of the last time she had done it, she
decided it was. As she prepared herself to absorb the contents of the
books' knowledge by magic, she thought, for a brief moment, that
she heard the dry rustle of pages turning in approval. She hoped she
was just imagining it.

Focussing on accessing the centuries of knowledge stored within
her grandmother's books, Holly released her witchlight into the
ether. A burning white light, sharply visible in the clear light of
day, poured from her fingertips and flowed away, outwards and
westwards, in the direction of the books stacked in Ninanna's
cottage. For a few moments, the light continued to flow outwards
and then, like a rip tide, turned and rushed back to Holly, bringing
with it the accumulated knowledge of Ninanna's personal library.
Ninanna's collection was huge, but nowhere near as big as the
library archives of the Coven. This time, Holly was relieved to
find the knowledge was not accompanied by the dry and dusty
whisperings that had invaded her head when she had absorbed just
part of the Coven's library. Sometimes, she thought she could still
hear them, but not now. The moment had passed in silence, and
Holly was left in a surprisingly dark kitchen that seemed empty
in comparison with the information now filling her head. Except

the kitchen wasn't really empty. Barny and Grindlebones were still there, sat side by side and observing her contentedly. And now Jake was there too, standing in the kitchen doorway and staring morosely at Holly. He didn't seem to be that contented at all.

CHAPTER 5

Jake was scowling into his coffee. He didn't have anything against the coffee. It was just that by scowling at it, he avoided scowling at Holly. He didn't really like being annoyed with her. He loved her, but these days (these days being ever since Holly had come into her full witchlight) there was a good deal going on around Holly that seemed to make him annoyed: annoyed or maybe scared. But, whatever the emotion, he was unable to express the full reason for it, and that just, somehow, made matters worse.

Holly, on the other hand, seemed to be having very little difficulty expressing herself,

"And so you see, with everything going on, the scattered nature of Brother James and the recent Coven visits, I really felt I needed to complete my exploration of Ninanna's books, just in case." Holly paused in what had been a full-on flow. Jake said nothing, so she continued, "I hadn't realised you would be home so early, or..." Holly's flow finally dried up.

Jake completed the sentence for her,

"...or you wouldn't have done it?"

"Or I wouldn't have done it quite so blatantly from the middle of this kitchen. I'm sorry. I know it gives you the creeps."

"It's kind of more than that, Prickles. Quite a bit more."

"More?"

"Yup."

Holly and Jake stared mournfully at one another. Barny and Grindlebones exited discreetly via the cat-flap.

Holly, as per usual, was the first to break the silence,

"I do try to be discreet, sweetie, but I am a witch. Magic is what I do. I can't just stop doing it."

"Can't or won't?"

"Both. As I said, it's what I do. It's what I am. Not doing it would be like denying myself, and that wouldn't be right."

"For you. It wouldn't be right for you, but what about me?"

"For me, or anyone close to me, in my view. If they loved me."

Jake found something annoying in his coffee again. Holly, exhibiting unnatural patience, just waited. Eventually, Jake looked up from his mug and carried on speaking as if there hadn't been a gaping silence,

"So, what did you find out?"

"Find out?"

"From your illuminating reading of your grandmother's books."

"Oh yes, well, not that much more than I had guessed already. Other than some technical detail about shape-shifting and animal borrowing, there was nothing that directly related to the current situation. Basically, it seems that Brother James had been in the back field and was almost certainly eaten by an animal or animals unknown whilst he was shapeshifting as a rabbit. Good grounds for never turning yourself into anything too low down the food chain."

"And…?"

"And, I shall probably check a little more thoroughly on Grindlebones and Barny, but there is already reasonable evidence to suggest they partook of parts of Brer James, though that, in itself, is not grounds for proving they actually killed him."

"Though they probably did."

"They are cats. He was probably a rabbit. They did eat that large rabbit the other night."

"Well, that's okay then."

"I didn't say it was okay, but it is natural."

"Yes, I guess it's about the only natural thing in this whole malarkey."

It was Holly's turn to scowl,

"Jake, sweetie, witchcraft and magic are natural for me. It's a genetic inheritance just like your blue eyes and black hair. It's simply that you're not used to it."

"And you are?" Jake's tone was decidedly and unexpectedly argumentative.

"Yes, I am. Now. It came as a shock at the time, a very big shock, but I've accepted it and adjusted." Holly paused, "I'm still adjusting, if truth be told. I can do almost anything I can think of, if I throw enough witchlight at it, and that's great in some ways. Amazing. But if you can do virtually anything, have anything, life risks becoming a bit purposeless, somehow. It's you that keeps me grounded, love, gives me a purpose, and keeps me going forward, if that doesn't sound too melodramatic. I do love you, you know?"

Jake remained silent for longer than Holly really wanted.

"I know, and I love you too, but your power, well, it scares me — scares me because of what you can do and I can't. Why love me when you can do anything, have anyone? These days, I kind of feel surplus to requirements."

"Oh darling, you're so not." Holly hurled herself at Jake and hugged him as tightly as she could manage given Jake's muscular frame and the foot's difference in their relative heights. "I love you for you, because you're you. I love you because what we have isn't related to magic. Yes, I probably could have anyone, but then they wouldn't be loving me for me. They'd be loving me because I'd compelled them, and that wouldn't be right or real. You were right when you said I could have anyone I wanted. I can. I do. I want you." At that point Holly kissed Jake, and for a while, all became right with their world.

"Shall we go upstairs, or do you fancy the kitchen table?" said Jake.

Holly looked at the hard and unyielding wooden surface of the otherwise very fine kitchen table and almost immediately magicked them both upstairs into the softer surroundings of the bedroom, but tactfully managed to restrain herself. Instead, she let Jake take her hand and lead her up the stairs to the bedroom, where they slowly undressed one another and then took their time exploring every inch of one another's bodies. Jake's body was wonderfully firm and lean from his outdoor veterinary work. The scars from the incident last year were, magically, barely visible. Holly enjoyed the feel of his firm flesh under her hands and then on top of her and then inside her.

After the extremely satisfying pleasure of their lovemaking, they lay side by side, skin by skin, in bed. For a little while, it was as if the negative elements of their recent conversation downstairs had never taken place. Holly's thoughts ambled leisurely and a tad soporifically from the pleasing firmness of Jake's flesh, to the delightful feel of the soft fur of the cats, to the sad and musty remains of the rabbit fur she had found in the field. At which point, her thoughts woke themselves up by wondering what Brother James had been doing in the field in the first place. It was, of course, possible that the man had had a bunny fetish, but there was no reason for him to have indulged his obsession in the field directly behind Holly's house when he could have picked any field anywhere in the country to do a Bugs in. It therefore seemed likely that he was there to spy on Holly and her nearest and dearest. The only real question was whether his motivation was personal or shaped by the Coven.

Holly rolled on to her side to stare casually up at Jake. He appeared to be drowsing deeply and very contentedly. Holly rolled back onto her back, stared at the ceiling, and carried on thinking.

The Coven. She didn't like what she had seen of it, but what she had seen hadn't actually been that much. Partridge had first introduced her to it via its mind-numbingly pedantic paperwork. The bureaucracy had repelled and worried her. Similarities to meticulous file keeping organisations like the Stasi had suggested themselves from the get-go. Then there had been the Coven's underwhelming lack of support during the issue with her grandmother, but that had been an absence rather than a thing she could get to grips with. It had painted a picture for her of the Coven's ways, but it was a picture with a large hole at its centre.

Since then, her contact with the Coven had been limited and piecemeal and seemed to involve them wanting things from her: her help in unblocking the Coven's ancient library and rectifying the damage caused during the prolonged fight between Holly and her grandmother; repeated invitations for Holly to come to work for the

Coven to "assist the Coven in its endeavours," and now demanding information about the last known movements of the apparently late Brother James. But for all that, what did Holly really know about the Coven? The answer was not a lot. Ninanna had held it in too much contempt to explain it in any detail, and Partridge had only ever told her things he felt she needed to know, but whether that was for her benefit or the Coven's, she wasn't sure.

Holly came to the conclusion that she was having problems working out what Brother James was up to because she didn't understand what the Coven was up to. At that precise moment, Jake woke up, stretched, and crawled reluctantly out of their soft, warm bed to go to the bathroom.

Holly watched him head-off as she was wondering what she could reasonably do to improve her knowledge of the Coven. She continued to watch him as he strolled back towards the bed, a contented smirk still on his face. As he moved past the bedside table, she noticed the book resting on it. It was a leather-bound edition from her grandmother's library, and it set her thoughts off at a tangent, along with the ubiquitous dry rustling. She blocked the latter. She reached for the book on autopilot just as Jake reached for her. He looked painfully dejected when he realised it was the book she was after, rather than his adjacent extremities.

"Sorry," said Holly, "but I wanted to check out the book." Jake said nothing, so Holly carried on, "It's books, you see, and libraries and the link between them and the Coven. I thought, maybe, I should pay the Coven a visit to ask for further access to their library so I can finish reading all the books. I thought the books and the process of engaging with the Coven might give me a better feel for the Coven and what it's really about."

Jake just looked even more baleful,

"But you've already absorbed their entire book stock into your witchlight, haven't you? What's left to read?"

"No, I haven't. That's kind of the point. Last time, it was just the books and manuscripts that dealt with Old Magic. I used my magic to sort them out from all the others and then absorb their knowledge. There are still stacks and stacks and stacks of books I haven't read, and who knows what I might find."

"You think the Coven's going to be leaving its secrets lying around on bookshelves?"

"Noooo, not really, but it may explain things, give me pointers, help me to understand better. Plus, it would provide me with a positive reason for connecting to the Coven, rather than the current negative ones. I really feel I need to do something, and taking a look at the rest of the books is something I can do relatively easily. I just feel an itch to go and see what there is to see."

"What, right now?" Jake managed to look alarmed, disgruntled, and annoyed all at the same time.

"No, not immediately. There's no rush. Why don't you come back to bed for a bit?" Holly patted the empty bed beside her in a way she hoped was inviting, but somehow the moment had gone, and they both knew it.

Jake shook his head glumly.

"I've got stuff to do too, Prickles," he said as he picked up his clothes from where they had been strewn around the room and started to put them back on.

Holly slumped back down on the bed, opened the book she was holding, and began reading. This time, the rustling in her head was completely audible. She was too upset to block it.

CHAPTER 6

Possibly because of Jake's sensitivities, possibly because of her own reluctance to engage with the Coven, several weeks passed before Holly made any sort of effort to seek access to the Coven's London-based library.

During the intervening period, Holly had not been troubled by contact from any Coven officials. At first she thought this was a blessing, but then she started to fret about what they might be up to whilst they were not making contact. The fretting grew steadily worse, becoming wrapped around the unknown nature of Brother James' activities at the back of her house prior to his demise and the exact nature of that apparently bloody demise.

At the beginning of March, spurred on by the thought that she was going to the Maldives with Sarah at the end of the month and didn't want to spend the whole of the holiday fretting about the Coven, or worse, constantly popping back half way round the world to check on what it was up to, Holly decided it was time to re-establish contact with the erstwhile governing body of British witchery with a view to returning to its library.

Magically secure in her Oxford cottage, Holly settled herself in the large, leather fireside chair, conscious that it was broad enough to block out views of the cottage beside and behind her from prying eyes. There was no need to provide the Coven with more information than was absolutely necessary. With reluctance bordering on physical distaste, Holly retrieved Brother Wainthorpe's calling card from where she had secreted it and used it to contact him.

The card was like a very thin and very immediate videophone. As soon as she touched the card and used her witchlight to reach out to its owner, a moving image of the Coven Inquisitor appeared across the card. Little seemed to have changed since their last meeting. He was wearing the same ubiquitous grey suit and dark tie combo apparently favoured by Coven men. Today, he appeared to be seated at a desk in an anonymously modern office. Judging from the skyscraper vista hazily visible through the large plate glass window behind him, the office was located within the financial centre of the City of London.

"Sister Beldam, what a surprise! What can I do for you today, or am I in luck and you are going to do something for me at last?" He ended the last phrase with a broad and overtly false grin. Holly produced a cold, thin-lipped smile by way of response.

"Brother Wainthorpe. As I hadn't heard from you recently, I thought I'd initiate contact. Is there any more news concerning poor Brother James?"

"Regrettably, Sister Beldam, there is not. His fate seems as uncertain, but ultimately final, as before. We still haven't been able to ascertain how he was transported from Oxfordshire to Cambridgeshire. We can find no evidence of him using his own magic to get from one place to another. Is there any more you can tell us that might help?"

Holly kicked herself mentally. What was the use of having exceptional magic power if she didn't use her brain with it? Why hadn't she thought things through properly and checked out the transportation angle? It was feasible that an unnaturally large and juicy rabbit had been caught in an Oxfordshire field by one or two expert feline hunters and had then been brought back to Basingfield by them. Perhaps Brother James had only intended to spy on her Oxford home and not on Jake and her in Cambridgeshire. The thought of him spying on her anywhere wasn't pleasant but hanging round the house he'd met her in was less intimidatory than apparently stalking her all the way back to Cambridgeshire. Conversely, it meant that either Barny or Grindlebones, or both of them, was guilty of killing... a rabbit. She was not sure, however, that the Coven would see it that way. It was probably best they didn't know about the boys' potential involvement in Brother James' disappearance and apparent dispersal.

Whilst Holly's thoughts were chasing themselves down rabbit holes that Brother James would never have the chance to explore, Brother Wainthorpe was waiting for a response,

"So, are you able to shed any light on how Brother James was transported between counties?"

Holly chose her words carefully, "I don't have any evidence that could help, I'm afraid."

"Oh well. So, if you've nothing new to offer us, to what do we owe the unexpected pleasure of this connection?"

"Well," Holly pulled her thoughts back into a semblance of order, "apart from enquiring after Brother James as a matter of politeness, I was going to respond to the Coven's often repeated desire to work with me and suggest a little project we could undertake jointly."

"Oh," it was Brother Wainthorpe's turn to pause and look somewhat bemused. "Well, I'm not sure, all things considered, that the Coven's going to be prepared to listen to a proposal from someone it's got under…" He paused again, but this time he appeared to be listening. As to what he was listening to, Holly had no idea. Perhaps it was the little man who lived in his head? Even when Holly enhanced her hearing to bat-like levels, she couldn't pick up the slightest trace of another voice. Yet, Brother Wainthorpe had now gone beyond listening and seemed to be having a conversation with an unknown other, "Well, yes, but… I see… Well… Yes, if you wan… I understand… Yes… Yes… No, I…"

Holly gained the feeling from the Inquisitor's tone of voice, and what she could hear of his end of the conversation, that someone was coming over all inquisitorial on him, and he wasn't enjoying the experience very much.

Holly sat and waited while the one-sided discussion continued. Eventually, to all intents and purposes, Brother Wainthorpe stopped talking to himself and re-established eye contact with Holly,

"I do apologise, Sister Beldam, that was exceptionally rude of me, but a representative of the Inner Coven wanted a word, and I could hardly refuse."

Holly didn't know if he could have refused or not. She had never heard of an Inner Coven before, but now that she had, her curiosity was pricked, both by the discovery of its existence and its obvious effects on Brother Wainthorpe.

"That's okay," she responded. "I wasn't too offended. Was it a helpful conversation?"

"Erm, yes, erm, very informative, thank you." The words stumbled out in an uncomfortable rush. "The Inner Coven is delighted that you are thinking of working with us and is intrigued by your proposed project. They would like to know more." Holly thought that, somehow, the words didn't sound like Brother Wainthorpe's.

"Oh good," she said, managing to sound as if she really meant it. "I'm delighted that they're delighted. How fortunate that they were listening in to our conversation. Is that normal, by the way? By Coven standards, I mean."

"Coven business is the Coven's business," said Wainthorpe as if he was chanting a mantra, but one with which he was not totally comfortable. What Holly couldn't work out was whether he was uncomfortable because eavesdropping was routine or because it wasn't. Holly made a mental note that this was something she needed to look into further and tentatively probed the calling card with an increased push of her witchlight to see if anyone else was "online." In response, she felt an unexpected push back, and the connection to Brother Wainthorpe suddenly snapped shut. The business card in her hand now looked like a plain and simple piece of card again. Moreover, when she tested it with her witchlight, that's all it was — a plain and simple piece of card. All traces of magic had completely vanished as if they had never been.

Holly didn't like being hung up on, so to speak. It was rude, and whilst that seemed to be par for the course with Brother Wainthorpe, she didn't feel he was responsible for the sudden termination of their conversation. The magic she had felt pushing back hadn't been his. She was sure of it. It had been surprisingly strong.

Holly's curiosity was now on overtime. There was the discovery of an Inner Coven, its eavesdropping tendencies, the presence of strong magic, and a sense of personal insult. As she could no longer use Brother Wainthorpe's calling card to make contact with him, she'd just have to pay him a visit in person. Well, there was no time like the present. She'd previously met the Inquisitor in the flesh and now had a very clear and current image of both him and his present location in her head from their recent and abruptly terminated conversation.

A brief moment's pause — combined with intense internal focus — and Holly was standing in front of a somewhat alarmed Marcus Wainthorpe. Even more alarmed were the five grey-suited and dark tie-wearing men in the non-descript office behind him. Sudden magical manifestation was clearly not the norm in Coven offices.

"So what, precisely, happened just then, Brother Wainthorpe? If it was intentional, I might just find myself insulted." Holly was determined to get her question in first.

"I don't know. I thought it was you who cancelled the connection."

"Well, I know that I didn't, and if it wasn't you, I'm thinking I'd like to meet the witch who did, because I'm beginning to find this entire situation rather rude and insulting."

"But there was only you and me connected," Brother Wainthorpe's words were hesitant, as if he did not seem especially convinced of his own statement.

"Come, come, Inquisitor Wainthorpe, we both know that isn't true. Coven business is the Coven's business, as you just told me."

"Yes, but…", but whatever Marcus Wainthorpe was going to say was lost in a loud pop, as a ball of cerise light appeared in the air between him and Holly, expanded in size and brightness, and then disappeared with an even louder pop, leaving within its place an immaculately turned out, glossily black-haired woman in a bright red suit and even redder killer heels. Smiling somewhat fixedly at Holly, she held out her hand,

"Caprice Graham, and you must be the infamous Holly Beldam. Pleased to meet you at last."

The witch was certainly direct. Holly both warmed to, and was slightly taken aback by, the lack of Coven formality and its insistence on Brother this and Sister that — but mostly Brother, if she thought about it.

Holly seized the extended hand as robustly as it had been proffered,

"Pleased to meet you, Caprice, though I admit to preferring the term 'famous' to 'infamous.' Slightly more positive connotations, I like to think. Not that I knew I was famous to begin with. So, what's your role in the Coven?" Holly waved her left hand to incorporate, rather broadly, the office they were all standing in.

"Oh, this is just the Inquisition Office," said Caprice, "merely a function within the service arm of our operations. It's not the main part of the Coven proper. The Inquisition's not the powerhouse it used to be. As for me, I guess I'm the "Go For" for the Inner Coven. Shall we walk and talk? I'm convinced there's lots to discuss." Whilst she was talking, she began to move away, gently but assertively drawing Holly along with her.

Holly glanced back to see how Inquisitor Wainthorpe was taking this double incursion into his office, along with the correspondingly swift exit. She was surprised to see expressions of what she took to be both fear and relief on his face. Somehow, she didn't think that, this time, either emotion related to her.

CHAPTER 7

Caprice Graham exited the Inquisition Office by its one and only door and walked briskly into a grey-walled corridor. Holly followed, not knowing quite what to expect. It was probably not the bland anonymity that greeted her.

The grey walls were unadorned: no paintings, posters, signs, or labels, just grey emulsion. The beige vinyl floor covering made the place seem institutional, like the goods inwards entrance for a large hospital. There were six doors on both sides of the corridor, all equally grey and anonymous in appearance. Caprice's colours of red and black stood out against the subdued tones like a shiny red apple in a bowl of over-cooked porridge.

The woman strode past all the closed doors without hesitation, heading purposefully towards the solid doorless wall at the far end of the corridor and then, without breaking her stride, walked into it, or rather through it. Holly hesitated briefly before following suit. Intellectually she knew that this was an accepted way for the magically gifted to access private areas. She'd experienced the same regularly when visiting the Coven's archive at the British Library, and at least one room in her Oxford cottage was accessed via a solid wall. Subconsciously, though, it still made her hesitate. Thirty-eight years of ordinary, magic-free life outweighed one and a half years of magical awareness, and just one year of full witchlight, every time.

The room Holly walked into was large, expensively furnished, and decorated primarily in black and white with an occasional slash of crimson. The floor was a chequer board of black and white marble. The furniture was highly polished ebony and/or black leather. A quartet of Rothkos in shades of black hung on the white walls, and five, four-feet-high Japanese pots were spaced around the room, their black glaze enlivened with deep crimson characters in Japanese script. There were no windows.

"Not much, I'm afraid, but it's my poor little home from home when I'm at work," said Caprice.

Holly stopped herself from laughing out loud at this failed attempt at understatement. The room must have contained a fortune of art and interior design.

"Nice," she managed by way of response.

"Have a seat while I fix us some drinks," Caprice gestured towards a spotless black leather sofa that reclined next to an ebony coffee table, so polished it looked almost like glass. Small off-white objects were arranged in an intricate spiralling pattern across one corner of the table. Holly had about thirty seconds in which to note that the objects were hand carved ivory miniatures — real ivory, and that she wasn't completely comfortable with this— before an expensive crystal tumbler containing a chilled gin and tonic, ice, and a slice of fresh lemon appeared in her hand.

"I get the feeling you're a woman who appreciates a decent gin and tonic," commented Caprice.

"Err, thank you," said Holly. "I do like a gin and tonic, though not normally before my morning coffee."

Caprice, holding a crystal tumbler that was a partner to Holly's, sat down opposite Holly on a matching black leather sofa.

"So…" she said, letting the ensuing silence rest expectantly in the air.

"So…" responded Holly and waited.

Caprice smiled. Holly smiled sweetly back. Caprice was the first to break up the accumulating silence,

"So what, exactly, brings you in person to the Coven offices, Sister Holly?"

"Just trying to make connections, Sister Caprice," responded Holly as she sipped at her G&T, "and, maybe, trying to fathom why an earlier connection with a Coven official I was talking to was suddenly broken. It felt a little… rude." She studied Caprice over the edge of her glass. The other woman displayed no physical reaction to the last comment.

"Broken connections are so annoying, aren't they? Faults will occur, even when magic is the telecom company, so to speak. I'm sure no insult was intended, especially to someone with your breath-taking level of power. It would hardly be sensible, would it?" Caprice continued without drawing breath, "Anyway, what was the project you mentioned to Brother Wainthorpe? I'm sure we'd love to hear more."

Holly wondered who the "we" in that sentence was.

"Was that why you chose to break the connection? If you'd wanted to learn more, I'd have thought that continuing to listen in on me talking about it to Brother Wainthorpe would have been a good way to do so?"

Caprice seemed remarkably unfazed by Holly's pointed questioning,

"The Inquisition are really only investigatory. They're not very good with new ideas or initiating things. They're more focussed on maintaining traditions and the status quo. Plus, they're only Coven servants, not the Coven, per se. The Inner Coven is delighted that you finally want to work with us. We've been hoping for a closer relationship ever since that unfortunate denouement with your grandmother. If I, or someone directly connected to the Coven, became a little over enthusiastic in my reaction to your news and inadvertently disconnected your connection to Inquisitor Wainthorpe, I can only apologise. But then again, it brought you to us in person, so maybe an apology is unnecessary."

"So, it had nothing to do with me attempting to probe the connection flow for, um, tributaries?" Holly's directness finally elicited a response from Caprice, who visibly winced.

"Oh no. Please don't think that. It had nothing to do with avoiding a deeper connection. I want that. The Coven wants that. That's why we are so pleased you are here in person and why I popped along to the Inquisitorial Office to find you."

Caprice smiled, almost convincingly. Holly continued to sip at her G&T while silently admiring Caprice's acting abilities. Caprice leaned forward across the coffee table, an expression of concerned remorse now fixed across her face,

"Please believe me."

Caprice was obviously expecting a response from Holly, which Holly declined to provide. The two women stared at one another over their drinks. Holly was reminded of a silent Mexican stand-off with added emoting.

It was Caprice who once again broke the silence. Suddenly sitting bolt upright, crossing her legs, and folding her features back into a bland and business-like simulacrum, she said, without any sign of her previous emotion, "Look, Holly, like it or not, we are the Coven. We govern round here. You have only recently acquired amazing Old Magic power, but sooner or later you're going to have to come on board with us. Given the recent issue over Brother James and his undoubtedly unfortunate, but still somewhat uncertain fate, we think it should be on our terms. So let's cut the crap, to use a phrase, and get down to proper business."

Holly counted to ten before replying. Maintaining eye contact with Caprice, she slowly placed her half-consumed drink on the spotless ebony table in front of her,

"Brother James' disappearance is nothing to do with me, though I would still like an answer as to what he was doing apparently hanging around my home in Cambridgeshire, given that our official meeting was several counties away. I remain prepared to talk to the Coven regarding a project I should like to initiate. That's why I'm here, but "terms," whatever they may be, have yet to be discussed, and I have some of my own. I see no need for things to be one-sided."

Caprice's posture became even more upright. "We are the Coven. Brother James was a servant of the Coven. We look after our own."

"Then you should be answerable for his apparent snooping around my private home and for whatever happened to him while he was doing it." Holly's hackles were rising, and the temptation to storm out of the luxury black and white box she was sitting in was strong. She realised, however, that indulging her temper was not going to win her access back into the Coven library. The way things were currently headed, though, it was difficult to see how she was going to get there legitimately. She gave it one last try. "Look, I'm really not sure where we are going with this, other than a repeat of a conversation I've already had many times with innumerable Coven representatives. I'm more than willing to "cut the crap" and any bureaucratic red tape, but please can we get down to business properly, without unnecessary and ineffectual attempts at leverage. You tell me you want to work with me. I am here, willing to work with you. Maybe we should just focus on the positive side of the equation?"

Caprice considered this for a moment, refolded her face into a look of happy enthusiasm, and said, "Well, what are we waiting for, Holly? Tell me your plans."

Holly held in check her surprise at this sudden mood swing and smiled somewhat weakly back at Caprice. She wondered where Caprice hid her personal on/off switch, but now was hardly a good time to ask. Instead, she took a small breath and calmly said, "I'd like to propose a small reading and cataloguing project."

"Sounds interesting," said Caprice, as if nothing of their previous conversation had taken place. "Want to tell me more?"

So Holly explained, matter-of-factly, and as if the tensions of the last ten minutes hadn't existed, that she would like to have open access to the Coven's library in order for her to read and absorb the texts that she hadn't been able to previously. In recognition of this freedom, she would provide the Coven with a catalogue of what she'd read.

"Magically, if you want, or I can feed the information into a computer database, or I can do both." Holly felt as if she was making a presentation to a funding committee, rather than to a representative of The Grand Coven of Great Britain, Ireland, and The Etheric Isles in Their Domain (to quote its full and ponderous title). It didn't feel like a particularly exciting proposal, but she hoped it might be of some limited interest to the powers that were. She knew from her previous times in the library that, somewhat surprisingly, there wasn't a clear ordered record of the books the Coven held.

The look of happy enthusiasm was still fixed to Caprice's face. If anything, it had grown happier and more enthusiastic as Holly was talking, becoming almost euphoric at the mention of a computer database. At best, Holly had expected a lack of interest in her proposal and, at worst, downright resistance. Caprice's apparent excitement at the proposed archival activities was peculiar, if not unnerving. Holly wanted to know what it concealed.

"What an absolutely super idea, Holly. No one has attempted to catalogue even part of the archive since the 1950s, and then it was never finished. The Librarian at the time developed a different agenda of his own and, obviously, that couldn't be permitted." The broad smile still stuck across Caprice's features didn't match the more sinister suggestions Holly was picking up from the concluding sentence. After ever such a slight pause, Caprice continued, "We really could do with getting the lower library back under control. I shall be delighted to notify the Coven of your proposal. I'm convinced they're going to be as excited by it as I am. You should have an official response within forty-eight hours. If it's a yes, as I'm sure it will be, you'll be invited to an informal gathering of Coven members — not the whole Inner Coven, obviously, but enough Elders to enable you to explain and expand upon your proposal in person before a final decision is reached. Right now, though, I'll wish you strong light and let you get on about your business. I'm sure you have lots you need to be doing." Caprice gestured to a space between two of the Rothkos on the solid back wall of the room, as if it was a door. Holly, taking the hint dumped in her lap, got up and walked purposefully towards the wall. Obligingly, a large, solid and black wooden door appeared in its midst.

"Once you are through the door, feel free to transport straight home. If you want, of course. There's no need to hang around the Inquisition offices unless you really want to, and there's no rule against transportation from the public parts of this building. So do feel free." Caprice smiled yet again.

Holly formed the distinct impression that Caprice wanted her to leave as soon as possible, so she exited from the black and white room, straight through the large black door and into the orchard at the back of her Oxfordshire Cottage. She turned round to look at the door, but it had already disappeared. Now, all she had to do was wait for the initial verdict of the Coven.

CHAPTER 8

The Coven verdict materialised a day and a half later.

Jake was, as ever, at work, and Holly was in the flag-stoned kitchen of the Oxfordshire cottage feeding the cats. She had taken to feeding them more frequently in the last few days. Not in the hope of fattening them up — they were exceedingly healthy and well fed — but in a, most probably, vain attempt to discourage the cats from self-catering with the assistance of the local bunnies. Given the likely fate of Brother James, Barny's and Grindlebones' enthusiastic hunting activities were, currently, a bit of a worry.

Holly had just deposited a fresh portion of cat food, as preferred by eight out of ten cats, in Barny's brown bowl, when a six-foot-wide by approximately three-foot-tall set of fluorescent green letters appeared in the middle of the kitchen about a foot above Holly's head height. Holly craned her neck upwards and read, "SISTER HOLLY BELDAM IS INVITED TO ATTEND AN INFORMAL GATHERING OF REPRESENTATIVES OF THE GRAND COVEN OF GREAT BRITAIN, IRELAND, AND ALL ISLES WITHIN THEIR DOMAIN, CURRENTLY TAKING PLACE, TO BETTER EXPLAIN HER PROPOSAL FOR READING AND CATALOGUING, BOTH APPROPRIATELY AND ELECTRONICALLY, THE COVEN'S ARCHIVE AND LIBRARY. RSVP WITH IMMEDIATE EFFECT."

The formality of the invitation had Holly in stitches, and the screaming capitals in her kitchen annoyed her. Nevertheless, she finished feeding Barny and Grindlebones and responded as instructed.

She had barely indicated that she was available and willing to attend when there was the usual loud pop and a ball of cerise light manifested in the centre of her kitchen. It expanded to form a standard-sized, door-shaped hole half an inch above the kitchen floor. In the witchlight doorway stood Caprice, who smiled — rather falsely, thought Holly — and held out her hand. Holly was taken aback by a portal opening directly within her house rather than outside it. It didn't seem to be in keeping with the ingrained etiquette of the Coven, let alone her own comfort levels. Nevertheless, she grasped Caprice's hand and stepped through the entrance.

Suddenly, they were both in a large, gothic, and extremely gloomy stone-built hall. Holly was further taken aback. She had expected either the bureaucratic anonymity of the Coven offices or the extreme luxury of a room like Caprice's. She hadn't been anticipating something that looked like a cross between the Renaissance Hotel at St. Pancras and Ely Cathedral. On second thoughts, more like Ely Cathedral. The hall seemed positively medieval.

The vast, echoing stone area was illuminated by a subdued light, reminiscent of candlelight, but no candles were visible. Rather, the high, stone walls themselves seemed to be emitting the light. The floor, which was not glowing, was covered in a black and white chequer pattern similar to, but less ostentatious than, the one in Caprice's room. This time the tiles were stone, possibly granite, rather than marble. The high ceiling was vaulted and appeared to be decorated with painted pictures and symbols, but Holly had no time to stop and consider them. The Coven representatives were waiting for her at the far end of the hall, and Caprice Graham was already with them. Holly hadn't noticed her transport herself across the distance.

Holly walked briskly across the wide expanse of stone floor. She had a gut feeling it would be deemed rude to transport herself in the way Caprice had done. Caprice obviously has a knack for dispensing with protocol.

A subtle smell of something rich, smoky, and multi-layered assailed Holly's nostrils: incense, she decided. The aroma, together with the sheer size of the space, emphasised the cathedral-like atmosphere, but, in Holly's experience, large stone churches were invariably cold edifices. This one was comfortably warm, as if somebody had set the central heating thermostat to the perfect temperature.

There were ten people waiting for Holly, including Caprice. As Holly drew nearer to them, she realised Caprice was the odd woman out, in more ways than one. The immediately obvious difference was the clothing. Caprice was once again wearing a bright red outfit, this time a scarlet dress and matching designer jacket with the same killer heels as before. The nine other coven members were uniformly dressed in black. Some wore suits with shirts and ties, others were more causally, but no less expensively, dressed in black sports shirts or jumpers and slacks, but everything was black. For Holly, this immediately recalled unhappy memories of her grandmother, Ninanna, who was a lover of expensive designer clothes, provided they came in a shade of dark.

Each member of the nine was also draped in a black robe. Holly felt that something monk-like with a cowl would have better suited the physical backdrop, but these gowns were more nineteenth century than twelfth and looked not unlike those sported by QCs and High Court Judges. Holly was interested to note that Caprice did not have a gown, but that wasn't the only thing she didn't have.

The nine gowned members were an interesting combination of ages and ethnicities. Witches didn't seem to like to show their true age, so the age span appeared to be twenty to a youthful sixty, meaning many, if not all of them, were actually much, much older. Ethnically, there was a multi-cultural combination of Asian, Afro-Caribbean, and Caucasian, but they were all, to a man, men. Holly wondered whether Caprice was the magnificent Queen Bee, surrounded by her drab acolytes, or whether, in truth, she was the feisty PA hired to create a certain image and brighten the place up. Either way, she seemed strikingly separate from the black-gowned male collective.

As Holly had made her way across the wide expanse of floor, the group had been standing and chatting amongst themselves, ignoring her approach. When Holly came up close to them, the nine men swiftly sat down on an arc of solid wooden chairs, all facing Holly. Caprice was left standing to one side.

The man at the centre of the arc cleared his throat loudly and, without looking at Caprice, said, "Sister Graham, please will you find Sister Beldam a chair and ask her to seat herself. Then you may perform the introductions."

Ah, the glorified and feisty PA, thought Holly. *Not an actual member of the Coven.*

A less than comfortable wooden chair materialised beside Holly. Odd-looking concentric circles were carved into the seat and back. Caprice indicated she should sit down.

"Sister Holly Beldam, may I introduce the Reviewing Panel who will be in charge of today's proceedings and who will be considering your application to the Coven. The Chief Reviewer is Elder Cavendish. Also present are Elder Brothers Godden, Cahil, Aashuri, Akuiji, Herne, Speedwell, Liu, and Lovelace. Me, you know. I will be assisting the panel in their deliberations, but I will not play a part in their final decision."

Holly hadn't met any of the men before, but she was getting the distinct feeling that, up until now, even during the follow-on from her fatal confrontation with Ninanna, she had only been dealing with lackeys, not the real power of the Coven.

"Good afternoon, gentlemen," Holly nodded broadly towards the arc of men arranged in front of her, "I hadn't realised I was making an application, as such. How exciting. I thought we were just going to have a mutual chat about my little cataloguing idea."

Elder Cavendish, who was seated in the centre of the arc of Elders, frowned. "The Coven has its proper procedures, Sister Beldam. We don't chat, and we don't do mutual. We judge."

Holly, for once, bit her tongue and didn't respond. Later, she wondered what had got into her to make her so circumspect, but at the time she justified it to herself on the grounds that she was still trying to be civil.

The panel commenced its formal assessment by asking Holly to explain her proposals from the bottom up, but her attempts to do so were constantly interrupted by comments of, "but we know that. Give us more detail" or, conversely, "but we know that. Give us less detail." Holly had already come to the conclusion that her plan was going nowhere and enough was enough when, Elder Aashuri threw in the following question, "Why should we trust you with our valuable archives given the potentially irreparable damage you caused when you slaughtered your own grandmother on our premises?"

Holly was so amazed by this outrageous verbal attack that she felt the need to take a very deep breath prior to launching a repost, but in the brief pause this caused, Elder Cavendish inserted his own question, " More importantly, Elder Aashuri, one should ask why we should trust an acknowledged murderer who is now implicated in the disappearance and likely dismemberment of one of our own Brother William James, an exemplary and loyal servant to this Coven and, ironically, a regular visitor to our fine library?"

To all intents and purposes, Holly remained calm and unflustered, but inside, her anger had already gone beyond simmering and was beginning to boil.

"Elder Cavendish, gentlemen, I am most emphatically not a murderer. Ninanna Beldam, my grandmother, was killed by me, yes, but in self-defence. I didn't take any delight in doing it. It was a grave, but unavoidable, necessity. Moreover, I have spoken at length and some tedium with Coven officials regarding, as I understand it, the largely still undetermined fate of poor Brother James. I am not involved in his disappearance, and the tone of your questioning is frankly extremely insulting. I have nothing more to say on the matter."

"Ah yes," a sickly smile spread across Elder Cavendish's craggy face — he was a witch who chose to appear a youthful sixty or so. "But your very unwillingness to speak further on the matter says so much, Sister Beldam. As an Old Magic practitioner and a very powerful one, we are led to believe, your apparent reticence and lack of insight into the sorry situation enunciates volumes. I find these volumes so much more interesting than the dusty old tomes you express such an interest in, and you, yourself are far more interesting than both."

The sickly smile became a smirk and quickly degenerated into a leer. At the same time, Holly had the distinct sensation that her bottom was being groped and that invisible fingers were working their way round to her groin. Shock and outrage gave way to concern that her anger had caused her to be so distracted that she had let someone, presumably Elder Cavendish, breach her defences. Moreover, she had the distinct impression that he was, somehow, actually groping her, rather than just causing her to imagine it. She didn't think he had the power to invade her mind, despite her anger having made her drop her guard. He was certainly managing to invade her physical space, though.

Holly focused her own power on the unpleasant sensations crawling across her right thigh and envisioned a stout wooden ruler coming down with a resounding thwack on the unseen fingers. She saw Elder Cavendish's features contort swiftly from leer to grimace, and the sensation of inappropriately probing fingers immediately ceased.

"I can see why you're not interested in dusty old tomes, Elder Cavendish. I would imagine there's insufficient porn on the Coven bookshelves to engage your warped little fantasies. I came here in good faith to discuss my proposal to help record and further restore the library I inadvertently helped damage last year. I don't glory in what took place between Ninanna and myself, but it was, very regretfully, unavoidable. I protected myself then. I will protect myself now. Please do not doubt it."

Holly was expecting Cavendish to back down at this point, but he did not respond as expected. She had become so used to Coven officials being wary of her not inconsiderable power that the bolt of dark green witchlight hurled directly at her by Cavendish almost caught her by surprise.

Fortunately, he drew attention to it first by yelling, "Do not profane the hall of the Coven with offensive innuendo, Madam, and do not threaten us!"

Despite her shock, Holly's response was decisive and quick. A ball of bright white witchlight surrounded the sizzling spear of dark green energy and had already tossed it back towards its maker before Cavendish waved his hands and extinguished the aggressive manifestation of his power. At the same time, the heavy chair Holly was sitting on was shoved violently backwards. Holly had to divert her own power to stop herself from falling and bashing open the back of her skull on the unyielding stone floor. She righted the chair before it had a chance to topple and was in the process of surrounding herself with a protective barrier of witchlight, before Cavendish could try any other tricks, when she sensed, rather than actually saw, nine diverse threads of vari-coloured witchlight attempt to snarl her own protective magic and pull it apart.

This was new to Holly, and she was not enjoying the experience. It required more effort than she was expecting to swat aside the individual rays of power. As soon as she disentangled one thread of witchlight, another took its place, and they just kept coming. Holly focused and sped up her response while exerting more power. And still they kept coming. Holly threw more of her power at the threads. She was at last gaining some ground and finding herself able to remove the entangling threads faster than they could reform. She had just removed the final thread when Elder Cavendish surged to his feet and shouted, "See how Old Magic insults the Coven! The witch has the temerity to rebut the power of the nine."

Holly was not sure where all this was headed, but she was not envisaging a happy outcome, though for whom, she was not entirely certain right now. She instinctively rose in response, but to her concern found herself dragged back down on her chair by an unseen power that was stronger than the previous nine threads combined. Yet, she could not detect any signs of witchlight at all and couldn't work out which of the nine coven members was behind it. What on earth was happening?

Holly directed her feral magic on the chair. Nothing. She carried on trying to free herself, rapidly and incrementally increasing the surge of power, but she remained stuck fast. This was not good. Sheer force of witchlight wasn't working, but as she could not work out who or what was holding her in place, she didn't know how to fix it.

"Not so powerful now, are we Sister Beldam?" This was Cavendish again. The other Coven members by now seemed to be in varying states of surprise and disarray, half in and half out of their seats. "The Coven is not without its own tricks and will not stand to be insulted by a neophyte witch, however powerful she claims to be."

Holly struggled to keep the lid on her anger and her growing fear. She had now realised two significant things. One, she had grown far too reliant on the sheer force of her own power overcoming all opposition and two, given the strength of the unknown power now restraining her, something subtler and more nuanced than throwing all of her witchlight at the problem was going to be called for.

Cavendish was clearly enjoying Holly's imminent defeat. He was positively strutting. The other Coven members, however, were exchanging glances and were visibly both shocked and worried by Cavendish's aggressive and adversarial approach. This gave Holly a different perspective on the matter and an idea. Looking Cavendish directly in the eyes, Holly said loudly and surprisingly calmly,

"And I did not come here in good faith to be insulted and physically molested by a dirty old man. Do the other Coven members know what you just did and that I was simply defending myself? Is copping a quick feel really an appropriate way for a Coven Elder to behave? What does that say about the rest of the Coven? Or is the insult to the Coven not so much mine as yours?"

Holly made sure she looked directly at each of the other Coven members as she said this. Then she developed her theme further: "May I remind you that I am a guest of the Coven. You have repeatedly invited me to work with you. You specifically invited me here today. Is it customary for the Coven to sanction the groping and physical assault of its female guests, or was it a dishonour especially chosen for me?"

By this stage of Holly's pronouncement, the eight other Coven members (Caprice was by now nowhere to be seen) had all risen fully from their seats and were talking hurriedly amongst themselves in an increasingly agitated manner. Then, Elder Aashuri appeared to make his mind up about something and, turning to Elder Cavendish, demanded in accusatory tones, "Cavendish, what have you done this time?"

Whatever Cavendish attempted to say by way of reply was drowned out by an increasing clamour and shouts of "shame," amongst other less-polite comments from the Coven Elders. It seemed Cavendish had something of a reputation. The more he tried to deny Holly's accusations, the more the rest of the Elders denounced him. It was almost as if they had been looking for an excuse.

In the ensuing chaos, Holly felt the unseen restraints that had fixed her to her chair melting away. It appeared her strategy had worked. She stood up rapidly and addressed the now arguing Coven members,

"Gentlemen, I will see myself out. I came here in good faith with a view to using my witchlight to our mutual benefit, but I have been singularly insulted. Whilst Elder Cavendish is most to blame, it appears that the rest of you knew of his proclivities yet gave him scope to exercise them. Shame on all of you, then. I intend to make sure that the witching community at large learns exactly what sort of men govern it."

Aashuri now took charge of the gathering, demanding silence from the rest of the Coven members,

"Enough. We have allowed things to get out of hand in more ways than one. Hecate knows what could have happened had things escalated further. Have we not learnt our lessons? We owe Sister Beldam a debt of thanks that she did not respond as she was surely entitled to do." It occurred to Holly at this point that he was not aware of the physical restraint she had been under. She filed it away mentally for consideration under calmer circumstances.

Aashuri walked towards Holly, his hand outstretched in a placatory gesture,

"We have not shown ourselves in a good light today. Please accept our genuine apologies, Sister Beldam. In recognition of the goodwill with which you came here and the appalling way in which you have been treated, I propose that we grant our valued Sister in witchlight full access to the library, as requested, to read and catalogue the many works we have stored there. Do I have your agreement, Elders?" There was the sound of at least seven affirmative comments. Holly didn't hear what Elder Cavendish's response was as he had, by then, been bundled to the back of the Coven group.

From behind the black-draped crowd of Coven members, Caprice suddenly remerged like a rising and determined red sun. A broad smile was stretched across her face,

"Leave it with me, my honourable Elders, and I will ensure that all is put in place for Sister Holly. She will have full access to the library as agreed. All I would ask, with your permission, is that she does not attempt a single full absorption of all titles in the way she did with the Old Magic books a while back, as it could be potentially damaging to the books. We are all aware, are we not, that there were, erm, traces left behind in the library after the last episode? I would also ask her to give us the benefit of the doubt on this occasion and not share her experiences here today too broadly." Caprice's smile grew even wider, to the extent that Holly wondered if her head was going to split in two.

Whilst fuming at her treatment and deeply troubled by the unknown power that had restrained her, Holly realised she had achieved her aim of gaining access to the library. Acceptance of the olive branch being proffered would buy her time to consider and analyse the incident in a calm and logical manner. She had to admit that some sort of breathing space seemed sensible. She therefore nodded to both Elder Aashuri and Caprice and accepted the offer and its accompanying terms, whilst biting back a number of sarcastic comments she was longing to hurl in Elder Cavendish's direction as the sounds of his unconvincing protestations of injured innocence once more reached her across the crowd of Elders.

CHAPTER 9

The unpleasant events at the Coven meeting left a surprisingly dark impression on Holly. It wasn't just the indignity of being groped. As a woman of some thirty-nine years' worth of experience, Holly had had the misfortune of being groped on all too frequent occasions and took great delight in applying hard elbows, raised knees, and the pointy end of an umbrella to the perpetrators whenever possible. It was more the underhand and insidious way that magic had been used to achieve what mere physical fingers could not. Then there was the realisation that maybe her witchlight was not as strong and impregnable as she had allowed herself to believe. And finally, there was the issue of what had held her on to her chair, when it hadn't appeared to have been either wild or standard magic and didn't seem to emanate from any of the Elders.

Whilst Holly gnawed away at these issues, she didn't feel able to share any of her concerns with Jake, given the tension between them and his ambivalence to magic matters in general. Sarah, of course, remained unaware of Holly's magic abilities, as did Holly's other mundane friends and family, including Holly's father. Yet again, Holly was forced to confront the fact that she knew very few people in the witching community, and no one close enough to confide in. Since the deaths of Partridge and Ninanna the previous year, she was, in fact, quite isolated from her fellow witchcraft practitioners. Or had she chosen to isolate herself? She had hardly been a joiner since coming into her light. That was another matter she needed to chew and fret over.

The planned holiday in The Maldives with Sarah proved a blessed, but temporary distraction to these anxieties.

Jake was, of course, more than happy to look after Barny and Grindlebones whilst Holly was away, thus saving her the task of popping back two or three times a day to feed them, as well as having to come up with creative reasons to explain to Sarah her repeated absences from the pool or beach.

Holly and Sarah flew out to the Maldives first class, drinking champagne all the way, which put Sarah in a particularly good mood from the outset. Sarah's expectations of the holiday were pretty uncomplicated, and Holly was happy to join her in the basic enjoyment of sun, sea, and sand, good food and exotic alcoholic beverages. Clear turquoise water and pale, soft sandy beaches were remarkably relaxing, and Holly had to concede that there was nothing like a tropical paradise for lifting your spirits and topping up your early spring tan, especially when a light dusting of witchlight turned out to be the best sun protection without inhibiting one's tanning possibilities.

The holiday away also provided Holly and Jake with some breathing space. Holly hoped the quiet and temporarily magic free environment would help Jake feel more at peace with things and maybe allow him to miss her a little.

By the time Sarah and Holly returned to the April dampness of the UK, Sarah was positively euphoric and Holly pleasantly chilled. When Jake greeted her return from the airport with the biggest and most passionate hug he'd given her in months, Holly was almost back to her old self. Their enthusiastic lovemaking later that evening fully reunited Holly with both Jake and her usual sense of well-being.

Holly's restored sense of positivity was in no way marred by the approaching imminence of her agreed cataloguing project at the Coven's archives. It was most certainly going to be a huge task, even with Holly's powers. It was, however, an itch she increasingly felt she needed to scratch. It would, she hoped, give her a much-needed sense of purpose, provide her with the opportunity to meet and mingle with other witches and, hopefully, enable her to add to her knowledge of the Coven. She also half expected — or maybe just hoped — it might enable her to work out what had so effectively restrained her in the great hall.

Caprice's requirement that she deal with each book or item individually, rather than magically absorb information en masse, exacerbated the size of the task, but even that did not irritate Holly too much.

She had agreed with Jake that she would treat the project as a long-term 9-to-5 task, meaning that she would be working on it when Jake himself was at work, leaving her free to spend a reasonable amount of quality time with him in a mundane fashion. She told Sarah she was doing some volunteer work, which was almost true and made Sarah feel good as she had been the one to suggest it in the first place. Also, as soon as she mentioned the word "archiving," Sarah lost all interest in what the work actually involved, which saved Holly the need to come up with elaborate subterfuges.

On Caprice's instruction, Holly had been provided with an outline plan of the lower library and a summary of what minimal catalogued information already existed. Using these documents, Holly had drawn up her own plan of how she was methodically going to work her way round the book and manuscript stacks. It wasn't going to be an exciting task, but, because of the potentially positive offshoots, Holly was feeling surprisingly upbeat as she approached London's British Library, the oblivious host to the Coven's own extensive library and record archive.

As had become something of a habit during the previous year, Holly first transported herself to an empty cubicle in the ladies toilets at St. Pancras Station. Leaving the less-than-sanitary delights of the toilet facilities, she walked through the station concourse, with its white columns and modern glass-fronted shops wrapped inside an old, historic building. She then walked out of the station and on to the busy Euston Road. Up the road a brief way was the British Library. She entered via the front gate, crossed the piazza in front of the building, went in via the main entrance, and followed the flow of visitors across the foyer, down a corridor, and into a darkened exhibition area.

While other visitors stopped to look at the manuscripts on display in the illuminated cases, Holly strode purposefully towards a very dark and anonymous corner of the room lurking behind an unprepossessing stack of plastic chairs. Placing her hand on the plain wall behind the chairs, Holly grasped the door handle that appeared, literally by magic, pushed open the previously unseen door it was attached to, and walked on through. Instantly she was gently floating down what seemed to be a lift shaft, except it didn't contain the usual clutter of cables, lift mechanisms, or an actual lift. Instead, the bottom of the shaft was carpeted in a thick, rich, deep red shag-pile. Once descended and standing on the carpet in question, Holly faced the nearest blank wall and walked straight through it into a reception area staffed by a small, dark-haired woman of indeterminate age wearing a pale blue top and what appeared to be a large snakeskin scarf. The scarf unwound itself, pointed its head towards Holly and hissed.

"Ssshh, Cyril, it's only Sister Beldam come to do the cataloguing," cooed the receptionist. The snake stopped hissing but continued to wind itself round and round its witch in an agitated fashion. "Sorry, I don't know what's got into him today. He's normally a very passive familiar, and it's not as if we weren't expecting you. We received the heads up from on high yesterday that you were coming." The woman rolled her eyes in a mock exasperated manner, but whether it was because of the agitated Cyril or the heads up from "on high" Holly could not be certain. "I'm Jemima Sheldrake, by the way, and I'll be your receptionist for today and the rest of this week." Holly resisted the temptation to crack a Beatrix Potter/ Jemima Puddleduck joke. "I'm actually the Head Receptionist and will be your initial point of contact whenever you are on site. That way, there's no need to bother the Chief Archivist and Librarian." Jemima winked conspiratorially at Holly, "The Librarian doesn't honour us with a visit all that often — or at all, really, if I'm honest." At the mention of the word "Librarian," Cyril increased the speed of his winding motions. Fortunately for the sake of Jemima, whilst he sped up, he didn't tighten up.

"I think I might have met the Chief Librarian last year, when I helped to re-open the library following the, err, incident with my grandmother." Holly suddenly felt very uncomfortable talking about the event and the damage it — or rather she — had caused. It dawned on her that this was the first visit to the archives she had made since the repair sessions, and she wasn't sure how she felt about that. Jemima, however, seemed unaware of any discomfort on Holly's part.

"Oh, I shouldn't think you did. He's a high up in the Inner Coven and doesn't get out of bed for anything less than a full Elder. I wasn't here last year myself, but I suspect it was just Coven officials who turned out for the repairs. Though I did hear it was all a bit tricky."

Holly felt unable to comment on the trickiness of it. At the time, she had dealt with things matter-of-factly, but now, being back in the same building was bringing things back to her in a way she hadn't anticipated. It was not the clean-up process that was troubling her, but the events that had preceded it.

"Well, I guess I ought to get stuck in. Those books and manuscripts aren't going to read and catalogue themselves." Holly was trying to sound both efficient and breezy, but she just wanted to get going.

"Of course. No worries. We are all really excited you are taking this on. It's such a relief, but I've got a bit of paperwork needs filling in and signing before you go through into the archive." The Coven loved its bureaucracy. Jemima handed over a three-inch thick wad of paperwork and a biro and indicated the empty chair and table over in the corner where Holly could sit to complete the necessary admin.

Holly took the documents with a sigh and sat down where indicated. There was a long list of dos and don'ts for users of the library, which Holly was required to sign to indicate she had read (and a duplicate copy for her to sign and keep should she need to refer back to check that she wasn't in breach of any of the don'ts). There was a disclosure form (also in duplicate) confirming she was an appropriate person to allow into the library and a disclaimer statement (likewise in duplicate) stating that the Coven would not and could not be held in any way responsible for any events — whatsoever and howsoever caused — that took place within the library and its environs. Finally, there was a lengthy document (this time in triplicate), already signed by Caprice Graham, setting out the agreed terms of Holly's cataloguing project to the effect that she could read, study, and absorb, or otherwise examine, all the books and manuscripts within the Coven's library on the understanding that she did so one at a time and that she would create both a magical and a mundane computerised record of every item she examined that would become the sole property of the Coven once completed. It managed to state this across seven densely typed pages (times three).

Holly completed and signed all the paperwork the requisite number of times and handed it back to Jemima in the hope and expectation that she could now proceed to the archive. The receptionist, however, felt the need to check that every page had been completed properly and that everything that had to be signed had been. Holly tried to curb her impatience, but Coven bureaucracy was wearing. She could feel her blood pressure steadily rising.

Eventually Jemima and, apparently, Cyril, were satisfied that the paperwork was in order,

"Thank you, Sister Beldam. You are now free to access the Coven's library and ancient archive." Holly made a move to go, but Jemima was continuing, "Please do remember that this is a library. Kindly respect other users by keeping any noise to a minimum and refrain from using all non-essential magics until you have vacated the building. Thank you for your cooperation. Do you know how to get to the old library and access its portal or would you like to see a seven-minute video explaining the process?"

Holly's growing irritation finally showed itself,

"I should think I bloody do know how to get into the library. It was me who basically re-built the portal." (*After I destroyed both it and my grandmother*, she thought but did not add). Cyril hissed defensively, and Holly at once felt guilty. "I'm sorry. It's not your fault. I shouldn't have sworn, but I undertook an immense amount of work here last year, without the need for any paperwork, I might add, and so I'm more than familiar with everything. I'd really just like to get started on my current task, please, if it's all the same to you."

Jemima nodded and silently pointed towards the door to the main records storage area. Holly wasn't sure if it was a sympathetic or dismissive nod, but she walked straight through the door indicated and into a huge maze of high shelving and narrow rat-run aisles. Every shelf was filled with files and boxes of files. The Coven generated a lot of paperwork.

Holly walked briskly down a line of shelving rat runs until she came to an open space between the shelves. A large, ornate pentagram was inlaid into the wooden flooring. The sight of the pentagram brought her up short. All she had to do was step forward, stand in the centre of the sigil, and transport herself. It didn't matter where, because, regardless of intended destination, she would automatically be delivered to the very centre of the library archive. There was only one way in and one way out, and it was via the centre of the pentagram.

Its design was more elaborate than it had been at the time of her confrontation with Ninanna. The original basic design had been severely damaged and in repairing it, Holly had added some embellishments of her own. Holly's toe traced the outline of a particularly intricate pattern contained within one of the points of the pentagram. If you knew what you were looking for, you might just make out an ornate P followed by something that might have been an M.

Holly recalled the carbonised outline of a sprawled human figure burned into the flooring at that precise spot, the place where Partridge Mayflower had died to buy her a few more moments of precious time in her flight from and eventual fight with her own grandmother. She blinked her eyes rapidly to clear them. She had mourned Partridge's death and still missed him, but now, when she had work to do, was not the right time to get tearful.

Irritated with her own unsettled emotions, Holly stepped briskly into the centre of the pentagram, transported and, as expected, found herself falling very slowly down a dark, narrow tunnel. Looking upwards, she could see the slowly diminishing opening that formed the centre of the pentagram. Around her, the darkness gave way to star shine, moving light that burned with a sharp, cold fire and a surprising twinkle of turquoise that she didn't remember seeing on past occasions. She glanced down into the darkness beneath her feet. Those feet would soon be making contact with the solid floor of the old library, but it was so dark she could see nothing.

The first you knew of your arrival was your arrival, but even as Holly glanced down, she saw an unexpected blob of pale turquoise light appear directly beneath her feet, expand in volume and brightness, and then disappear again with a *poof!* she sensed rather than heard. The blackness resumed momentarily, and then a dull glow just about managed to illuminate a small area of the library floor and the thick auburn hair of someone standing on it. The person below looked up, and Holly saw a pale face topped with the same auburn hair. Impossibly it looked like Partridge Mayflower. Then the light and the face disappeared, and it was dark once more. Holly found herself standing on the unseen but solid floor of the library.

CHAPTER 10

Holly stood perfectly still in the dark: partially in shock, partially in case she could hear anything, the slightest, smallest, anything that might indicate there was someone else in the library besides her. Logically, she knew that the someone could not be Partridge. He was dead — very dead — but she had just seen him looking up at her. It was almost the reverse image to her last memory of him alive, when she had watched his silhouetted figure growing smaller and smaller as she had descended from the pentagram to the library and he had remained waiting above to protect her. The protection had been short-lived. Then there had been the sad, carbonised outline of a sprawled figure burned into the flooring, like a negative crime scene outline, which, Holly felt, it surely was.

Holly listened. The only thing she could hear was her heart beating far above its normal rate. She consciously slowed it. The beating grew calmer and quieter, but there was no other sound to be heard.

In the silent dark, vivid memories ran a gut-wrenching film show through Holly's mind: Partridge's patient mentoring of Holly as she first discovered her witchlight; his support for her, despite the cold indifference of the Coven, when things came to a head with Ninanna; their final meeting in the library, by the wooden pentagram, as Holly went down into the old archive in the hope of finding something with which to defeat Ninanna and prevent her from harvesting the murderous power she had been accumulating and for which she coldly intended to kill Holly.

"You'll come straight down after me?"

"No. I'm going to stay here and watch your back."

Partridge had stayed and faithfully guarded her back for as long as he lived, which, because of Ninanna's spite, was not that long. The film show cut back to the carbonised outline of Partridge burnt into the flooring of the upper library.

At that moment, the lower library's own illumination system began to come on. No longer the exceedingly dull glow that for many years used to illuminate the shelving (though illumination had probably been too strong a term) and that had apparently highlighted the red headed man looking up at her just now, but a flush of white light that lit up the book stacks like a clear summer's morning. Holly had certainly left her mark on the library when she helped to restore it.

Holly saw row after row of bookshelves stretching out radially from the centre of the library and finally fading beyond the reach of even Holly's summer morning lighting scheme. It was going to take forever to search the endless rows for just one person. There was no point in even trying. She could however, she realised, run a tracer spell.

The possibility hadn't immediately occurred to her — though it should have, she screamed at herself, it should have — because it was a pointless exercise running a tracer on someone who was long dead and whose physical remains were equally long gone (unlike Brother William's). Now she thought about it, though, it suddenly seemed the obvious thing to do.

Holly decided she wanted to search out Partridge Mayflower within the labyrinth that was the Coven library. She focused her will on the activity, and the search immediately began. Nothing. She repeated the exact same process but intensified the flow of her witchlight. Still nothing. She repeated the process a third time, but the answer came back the same. There was no physical trace of Partridge Mayflower within the subterranean library. Yet, she was sure she had just seen someone, and that someone looked just like Partridge.

Holly repeated the search yet again, but this time not specifically for Partridge. Instead, she sought out any living being in the library other than herself. After three more fruitless attempts, the answer was as negative for any and all humans as it had been for Partridge. The only living things in the library were Holly and a colony of cockroaches, which were resident somewhere on the far edge of the book stacks.

And yet, she knew she had seen Partridge looking up at her, or at least someone who looked like Partridge — really like Partridge.

So what to do? She had come to the library to start work on the cataloguing project, but how was she going to be able to settle down to routine sedentary work knowing that Partridge was here. Except, of course, he wasn't. Her witchlight had proved that, but she knew what she had seen. And yet… Holly's mind was spinning viciously in on itself.

Holly knew Partridge was dead. She had seen what little Ninanna had left of him spread-eagled on the upper floor. He had been dead for over a year.

If she hadn't seen Partridge — if Partridge, or anyone else, come to that, wasn't here — then what had she seen? The ever-decreasing circles in her head carried on decreasing. What was going on here? Why was her mind choosing to play up now?

"Because," said a dry, rustling voice in her head, "the dust has settled, so you can see more clearly. Also, you have returned. We are once again at home here."

With a jolt like an electric shock, Holly was finally obliged to confront what she had been pushing to the back of her mind all the last year: the papery rustling that had first joined her thoughts when she had drained all the books on Old Magic in the Coven's library. Centuries worth of thoughts, opinions, and knowledge, mixed with spent witchlight and built up organically over time. She had thrust them to the back of her mind when she had returned to the library last year to help unblock and restore it. There had been more than enough to think about at the time, and it had blotted out the rustling. She had largely learned to ignore the rustling ever since. Now, here she was, back in the centre of where it all started — or finished, depending on how you looked at things — and the voices, it appeared, were much stronger in their place of origin. They were clearly not willing to be overlooked any longer.

Suddenly, it was all becoming too much: the pressures of the last year, seeing Partridge (or not), the voices in her head. Holly felt she was losing control of matters in general and herself, in particular.

She didn't hesitate. She took a few, rapid steps back to the spot where she had arrived in the library and transported herself.

The fall back up the tunnel of starlight was painfully slow, but she could sense the voices growing fainter, and that, in itself, was a relief. There seemed to be no awareness in them that she was leaving. The sentient voice that she had heard just now made no comment. Holly took calming deep breaths as she continued to rise, and then she was back up in the middle of the wooden pentagram and walking past the shelves, and to the door, and out.

As she passed Jemima, Cyril hissed, and Jemima managed a brief, "That was quick."

But Holly kept on going, throwing back an equally brief, "Something's come up. Got things to do. I'll get back to you. Strong light." And then she was rising up the lift shaft and through the British Library and out into the almost fresh air of a London morning.

Would she be coming back? She had no idea.

CHAPTER 11

Holly's sudden and unexpected departure from the library caused a brief and shallow ripple in the otherwise largely gossip-less working lives of the library's staff and an even less noticeable vibration in the organisation's operational procedures. Jemima tutted. Cyril half-heartedly hissed. Routine continued. Readers came and went infrequently. Files needed to be found and books returned.

Jemima called one of the library admin staff over from the back office, "Finton, this illustrated grimoire needs returning to the under library now that Sister Patel has finished with it. Would you mind, please?"

Finton grunted.

"Please?"

"I'd obviously prefer not to, at the moment."

"You and everybody else, but the book still needs returning to the under library. It's too valuable and volatile to leave lying around up here."

Finton, never a joyous man at the best of times and one of the older members of staff, looked even more hangdog than usual. His familiar, Petrus, poked his head out of Finton's jacket pocket and peered up at his witch. They exchanged a look. Petrus twitched his pink nose, but as he was a rabbit, this was hardly unusual.

Finton held out his hand towards Jemima, who placed the grimoire in it.

"Thank you," she said and immediately resumed her scrutiny of the pile of printed forms in front of her.

Finton, with Petrus still snuggled in his pocket, trudged reluctantly towards the pentagram portal. He wasn't a happy bunny, metaphorically speaking. Petrus wasn't, literally.

As the pair of them descended through the night-time of the portal, the grimoire held firmly in Finton's left hand, a puff of dust billowed across the floor in a distant part of the lower library and then settled.

Finton and his rabbit were almost at the end of the portal descent when another puff of dust began its small journey across a different section of the lower library floor. It dissipated and settled in the exact spot that, fifteen seconds later, was filled by Finton's brown brogue encased feet and, above them, the rest of Finton.

The witch and his familiar made their way briskly through the shelves and book stacks of the lower library. Their journey was illuminated by the light of a clear summer's morning. Finton was constantly looking back over his shoulder for something, but whatever it was, he clearly did not see it. From time to time, a small swirl of dust billowed against the base of yet another book stack, but Finton didn't notice.

Eventually, Finton and Petrus arrived at the set of shelves that was their intended destination. They stopped. Finton lifted the grimoire and placed it on a shelf just above his head.

Lowering his arm and starting to turn around with a view to exiting the lower library as soon as possible, Finton suddenly found himself standing in front of a short, seemingly middle-aged woman wearing a rather old-fashioned grey wool suit.

"Sister Echinacea, how are you today?" Finton's voice managed to force itself into tones of excessively effusive bonhomie within the confines of the brief day-to-day greeting.

The woman said nothing, just smiled enigmatically.

"Well, you are looking good, I must say, seeing as you've been dead for the last —what is it — twelve years?"

The woman smiled again and disappeared.

Finton pulled out a crisp white lawn cotton handkerchief from his top pocket and dabbed distractedly at his forehead and the back of his neck, where he had suddenly broken out in a cold sweat. Petrus had retreated into the depths of Finton's jacket pocket. The only visible parts of him were the tips of his twitching white ears.

Finton walked as quickly as he could — without resorting to running — back towards the bottom of the portal. Petrus remained curled up nervously in his pocket. From time to time, little puffs of dust swirled around Finton's retreating feet. In his hurry, he did not even notice them.

Though it seemed like an unusually long walk back, Finton reached the portal entrance in record time. The whole time, his thoughts had been split between getting back to the portal and when and where he'd last seen Sister Astarte Echinacea alive and breathing. In relation to the latter, it had been a long time ago and part of a past he had almost forgotten. He preferred it that way. If the past was another country, he had no desire to play even the occasional tourist.

Finally transporting himself and Petrus into the portal, Finton let out a gut-felt sigh of relief. Down in the lower library, with another puff of dust, something sighed too.

CHAPTER 12

As soon as she could after her sudden departure from the library, Holly transported herself home to the domestic security of her Cambridgeshire house. She needed space and time to think. First and foremost, she needed a strong cup of tea and a hug. Magic swiftly provided the former, and Barny supplied the latter. Though, in order to achieve the required cat hugging experience, Barny had to be transported from the shady patch of thick undergrowth he had been occupying whilst staking out a rabbit-run and relocated in the kitchen at Basingfield Lane. Holly's beloved familiar was not best pleased to be dragged (magically or otherwise didn't concern him, it was the indignity of the without-his-leave relocation that annoyed him) from a morning's leisurely contemplation of lunch into the midst of an emotional need-fest. But once he sensed Holly's real need, he was more forgiving. With little more than a mild feeling of resignation, he gave into the liberty of fierce cuddling he permitted no one but Holly.

Two cups of Earl Grey tea and a prolonged hug-a-thon later, Grindlebones strolled unsuspecting into the kitchen and was somewhat surprised to be scooped up by Holly, unceremoniously dumped on her lap next to Barny and despite, or because of, the lack of room on the said lap included in an armful-of-cats squeeze. He had the grace and maturity not to demonstrate his surprise via the time-honoured feline method of squirming and sharp claws. But, as soon as dignity and Holly permitted, he vacated the lap and left Barny in sole possession. He really felt it was Barny's responsibility to indulge Holly in her ongoing need for an armful of soft, warm fur and loud, throbbing purring.

Holly was finally feeling less agitated than when she had first fled the library. For starters, she was prepared to admit to herself that "fled" was the appropriate word to use to describe her departure. But the cause of her departure still concerned her. What had happened back there? Either her mind was playing tricks on her, or the residual imprint of the library itself was, and neither was a comforting option. The fact that the residue in her head was capable of attempting a conversation and might be developing a mind of its own inside her mind was even less of a calming prospect.

Perhaps it was only to be expected that she would be stressed going back to the library for the first time since the post-fight clean-up operation, but was she really so stressed that she would hallucinate seeing the dead-without-a-doubt Partridge? Plus, there was that voice in her head.

Okay, since she was in the mood for admitting things to herself, she had been consciously ignoring the rustling in her head for months. She had known, more or less, what it was, and right at the beginning of the confrontation with Ninanna it had proved invaluable. But Holly had spent all of her life up until that point being alone in her own head. The presence of others — or at least something else — had been disturbing. She had blocked it, and the more she blocked it, the easier it had become to pretend to herself that it wasn't there. Perhaps she should have anticipated a reaction when she returned to the library. Perhaps she always had. Or something had. Maybe that was why she had felt the need to return to the library? That was really worrying. If that vision of Partridge was just an hallucination, it meant she was no longer totally in control of herself. But if the voices had lured her to the library, didn't that mean that something else was in control?

Holly was also very conscious of two other matters she hadn't given enough consideration to since the previous year.

When Partridge had first taken her to the old library, as opposed to the mind-numbingly bureaucratic records maintained by the Coven in the archive above it, he had said there were echoes of Ninanna's cottage in relation to it. It had grown to accommodate the books and manuscripts it housed and was now bigger inside than when it was first built (the outside hadn't changed any). Ninanna's cottage was bigger inside than out because it was built on Old Magic. Did that mean the library was built on Old Magic too? Holly had become the go-to-gal for all things Old Magic, so why didn't she sense it in the library? And if it wasn't Old Magic that shaped the library, what was it? Was there something out there that she knew nothing about, like the restraining presence she'd felt in the Coven's hall?

Then there was the issue of something that lay within the Old Magic of what was once Ninanna's, and was now Holly's Oxford cottage – the physical remains of Ninanna herself, stored safely and securely in the centre of a restraining pentagram and, as an extra precaution, beneath a heavy-duty guarding spell. The remains were intrinsically linked to Holly's family-sized Old Magic, because that's what it literally was – family-sized. Ninanna had collected the power from her entire family and anchored it to their physical remains and the Moonstone ring Holly was wearing. In killing Ninanna, Holly had freed her family and had caused the power to be suspended between two familial nodes — the first of the line and the last of the line. Holly was the last of the bloodline, and Ninanna had been the first, the head of the family (or what was left of it). Now, Holly wore the Moonstone family ring as head of the bloodline (not family — there was no family left to be head of). And the other end of the vast vibrating wave of Old Magic she had inherited, was her late grandmother's earthly remains. From time to time, she had wondered if she had heard sounds from the other end of the connection. What if more of Ninanna's consciousness remained than Holly had judged? Could she be the source of the incident in the library and maybe even the one in the Coven hall?

No, Holly berated herself, that was just her paranoia speaking. She needed to get some perspective. As comforting as Barny's furry warmth was, she needed to talk things through with a logical, verbally communicative human who knew about her witchlight. Trouble was, she wasn't sure Jake would be up to that. He wasn't exactly warm towards all things magical at the moment. If she was being honest with herself, Holly wasn't sure that he was all that warm towards her at the moment, but now wasn't the right time to unpack that emotional nest of vipers. Then again, Holly wasn't sure that there was ever going to be a right time.

What was happening to her life? A year ago, she thought she'd got it all sorted. She had protected those she loved, come into a witchlight startlingly brighter than anyone expected, and was able to do virtually anything she could think of. She and Jake appeared to have an equally bright future ahead of them: loving and passionate and with no material difficulties to get in the way of their domestic bliss.

Holly permitted herself a flush of warm fuzziness as she remembered their early times together: the uncomplicated physical pleasures of Sunday morning lie-ins with Jake, including, post lovemaking, two piping hot mugs of strong black coffee and a large plateful of bacon sandwiches shared between them. Then there had been their closeness as Jake recuperated from Ninanna's attack on him. That had had its dark side, though, so perhaps that wasn't the best memory to summon up. Still, Holly could vividly recall Jake sitting reading in the cottage's summery garden, propped up against a cluster of cushions and pillows and with his feet resting on an elegant nineteenth century footstool. A little later, the footstool had been used creatively when Jake and Holly put Jake's recovery and re-developing physical stamina to the test. Holly smiled broadly to herself at the pleasure of that particular memory.

So why were she and Jake so distant these days? Why didn't the Coven just leave her alone? What had really happened in the library? Why did she only think in questions, but no longer know the answers to anything?

Any good the cats and the Earl Grey had done dissipated like steam from a cooling kettle. Holly placed both her arms in front of her on the kitchen table and slumped forward on to them. Jake found her in exactly the same position over an hour later.

"Holly, are you all right?" Jake called gently from the kitchen door, but there was no response. "Prickles, are you awake? What's up?" Jake stepped forward and crouched down beside her, placing his arm across her shoulders. "Prickles?"

Holly raised her head long enough to show Jake two very pink eyes in a puffy, tear-stained face and burst into tears again, producing big, heaving, air-gulping sobs. She hadn't cried like this in over a year, possibly longer. Whilst Jake took a deep breath and wondered what to do next, Holly flung herself into his arms and carried on crying. Jake hugged her tight and stroked her hair, still without an idea what to do.

Barny and Grindlebones emerged from the shadowy recesses of the kitchen and sat down under the kitchen table on either side of Jake and Holly. Both tucked their front paws under their chests, shut their eyes and waited. They didn't have long to wait.

Holly raised her head, took a deep, somewhat snotty, breath, and splurged, "I need help, Jake. I went to the library. I went back down to where it all happened, and I saw Partridge. At least, I think I saw Partridge. But possibly I didn't because, of course, he's dead, and the books are talking to me in my head again, though I guess they didn't really ever stop. But now it's louder and more coherent. There's stuff going on with the Coven, including strange magic I don't understand. But possibly I should, because it may be Old Magic, but then again, I don't know anything about it, so perhaps not. I thought I could deal with the Coven, but after what happened, I'm not sure I can. But I have to, because I have to protect Barny and Grindlebones and you. I have to protect you too. Sorry, but it looks increasingly likely that Barny and Grindlebones may have eaten Brother William, although I'm sure they did it by mistake. It was only natural, because he was probably a rabbit at the time, but the Coven won't understand. I'm not sure I fully understand, but most of all, I don't understand what's happened to us. You and me. We were so close, and I love you so much, but we've become distant and I can't talk to you about magic, though it's my life now and I need to talk to you about my life, because I want it to be your life too, so I need to, but I can't. So, what am I going to do?" Holly took a huge breath and stopped the splurge. Her wide, hazel eyes, which currently looked more red than brown, stared up at Jake pleadingly. Under the table, a pair of green eyes exchanged equally wide-eyed non-verbal communication with a pair of saffron-yellow ones.

The silence that briefly filled the kitchen was thick like freshly cooked, warm dumplings. Then Jake scooped Holly towards him and held her tight against his chest. Holly burst into tears yet again, but in a good way. And so did Jake.

When they had both got their tears under control, Jake stood up, held Holly by her shoulders and at arm's length and looked directly down into her tear-stained eyes,

"Prickles, other than that last bit, I have, thankfully, absolutely no idea what you are talking about. The last bit you and I can cope with. The first bit, because it seems to be about magic, or may just be a bad dream, who knows, is something I have every faith that you will deal with, once you've thought things through calmly and logically.

"I'm going to be brutally honest, love, magic scares me. Your magic scares me… a little. The magic of others and this whole Coven thing scares me a lot. I end up feeling weak and powerless, and that's not how I like to feel. I don't know how you cope with it or have adjusted to it so quickly and so well. I don't know why you choose to stay with me when I have no magic, and you could go anywhere and do anything. The only thing I do know is the magic — this witchlight you have — is part of you and is very powerful. You are very powerful. You have found a way through situations before and can do so again. I have faith in you and, yes, in your magic."

He paused briefly, but only briefly. Holly had no time to take a breath, let alone say anything before he continued,

"The fact that someone as powerful as you loves me enough to ask me what to do makes me feel a little bit better about myself. Admittedly, in a weak, ineffectual, non-magical sort of way. But I'm clinging to the feeling good bit, because I like feeling good and maybe I haven't been feeling that way so much recently. But now, I'm at risk of blabbering, so, in a calm, measured, and structured way I'm going to say this: one – I have faith in you and your magical ability to sort things out, whatever the things that need sorting out may be; two – I will admit to having hang-ups about the magic which I, *I,* please note, have allowed to get in the way of us. With your help, I think we can talk about those hang-ups. It may take a while, and we will need to be a whole lot calmer and more logical than we are now, but given time and patience I believe we can work through things and come out the other side, stronger.

"In the meantime, I will be here for you, non-magically, while you sort out whatever it is you need to sort out with the Coven and the library and... the rabbits? If nothing else, I can hold the tissue box for you when you need it, though I can see you've already magicked one up for yourself." Jake paused to hand Holly one of the tissues from the box that had just materialised in front of her and which she was clearly starting to need again. "The only thing I can't do is get involved in the magic side of things. I don't have the knowledge, I don't have the power, and I'm scared shitless by the little I do know. So, please keep the magic side of things away from me and do what you need to do to protect me, as well as these two feline lads who appear to be sitting sentry duty on us. That way, we'll all be fine." Jake nodded decisively at Holly, then bent forward and kissed her on the top of her head.

Holly hugged Jake robustly by way of response. In some ways, she felt comforted by his speech. She mentally corrected herself — in *most* ways she felt comforted, and she was grateful that Jake had finally opened up to her about his fear of magic. But, as understandable as it probably was, she wished he didn't have it. That he had such faith in her magical ability was wonderful. That he wanted as little as possible to do with the witchlight that was an integral part of her, was not.

Holly took a deep, purposeful breath,

"Okay. I am getting myself back under control, I think. Tomorrow, I'm going to go back to the library, calmly and rationally, to look into things properly. I will take all necessary precautions in advance and go prepared, and I will work out what is going on in my head and in the library, and I'll deal with it. I might even start the actual cataloguing project at the same time. The monotony should be calming. How does that sound?"

"That sounds like my girl," Jake smiled reassuringly, "but before then, why don't we get some dinner on? I'm starving. And why don't we prepare it together, the old-fashioned way, with peelers and knives and other appropriate kitchen utensils, rather than magic? It might be fun." Jake looked expectantly at Holly. She smiled back. If the smile was a little hesitant, Jake didn't seem to notice.

CHAPTER 13

The following morning, Jake and Holly were both more than a little tired. It had been worth it, though. First, there had been the well-cooked and very satisfying meal. Then, it had been a wholly satisfying night, emotionally and physically. As a result, neither had had much sleep. Nevertheless, the two of them got up bright and early, and with wide smiles spread across both their faces, to make their preparations for a solid day's work: Jake in a broad green field with a herd of Charolais and Holly in a library with no natural light and a head full of issues.

Jake was the first to leave the Cambridgeshire house. On the way out, he stopped at the front door to pull on his waxed cotton jacket and his Wellington boots.

"I'm off now. I should be back around six-thirty to seven tonight. Will you be home by then?"

Holly grinned. "Of course. I'll make sure I'm home at the same time as you. It doesn't exactly take me long to get back."

Jake's own grin collapsed into a suddenly more serious expression, "On that note, I don't know if this is the right time, but I've been meaning to ask you something. Would you mind going to your Oxford place before heading off to the library, or anywhere else, really? And can you come back here via Oxford? I think I'd feel safer if your magical vapour trails didn't lead straight to our home."

His request startled Holly. It made no sense magically, but she agreed to it because she wanted him to feel safe and she didn't want to jeopardise last night's happy-glow feeling. It sort of worked. Jake's grin returned, albeit with a slightly sheepish tinge to it. Holly, however, left the Basingfield Lane house in a more subdued manner, exiting slowly on foot via the back door, through the back garden with its abundant display of spring flowers, up over the fence, across the greenly sprouting field at the back of the property, through the blossom-filled orchard at the foot of the cottage's garden, up the path running through the equally verdant spring garden surrounding the cottage, and into the black and white Oxfordshire cottage itself via its solid wood back door.

Holly stayed in the cottage long enough to grab a cup of hot, fresh coffee and make sure that both Barny and Grindlebones were inside the cottage, soundly asleep in close proximity to the soporific warmth of the cottage's Aga. How long they would stay there was another matter. They were cats, with pressing cat imperatives. But then again, those imperatives usually involved extended periods of comfy sleeping, so perhaps they'd stay put for a while. Then, with a resolute intake of breath, Holly transported herself to the ladies toilets at St. Pancras station.

The brief walk up the rush-hour-clogged Euston Road to the British Library seemed to take less time, but be more onerous, than usual. By the time Holly had walked through the imposing library gate and across the wide plaza in front of the library building, she was coming to the rueful conclusion that it was her own head, rather than any external magics, that was the cause of her problems. She took another deep breath, told herself firmly to take herself under control, and marched purposefully through the library to the discreetly lurking non-lift, sailed down the lift-empty lift shaft, and through the wall into the Coven's archive and library.

Jemima and Cyril were in exactly the same position as the previous day. Jemima had merely exchanged a pale blue cotton top for a pale pink silk one. Neither she nor Cyril showed any sign of surprise at Holly's return, though Cyril hissed as Holly approached the reception desk. Jemima simply said, "Good morning, Sister Beldam. Will you be staying longer this visit?"

Holly briefly nodded, "Hopefully. Something unexpected cropped up yesterday, but today I'm all about the research." Cyril hissed again. Holly liked to think it was a hiss of approval, but she wasn't really sure.

Second time around there was, at least, less paperwork to complete. Holly only had to sign herself in, and she was once more walking down a line of high shelving rat-runs and into the open space where the ornamented pentagram was waiting. This time she made a point of standing by the tip of the star where the P and M were woven into the complicated design. Crouching down, she traced the elaborate letters with the end of her left index finger. She thought long and hard about Partridge, who he had been, how he had died. She could imagine him saying, "No need to get maudlin, girlie. It was my choice." But she knew it was simply a combination of memory and imagination. There was no trace of Partridge in the pentagram or in the library as a whole that her discreetly probing witchlight could detect.

Satisfied as much as she could be, Holly stepped into the plain centre of the pentagram and transported. As before, she found herself falling very slowly down a long, dark tunnel. This time, she didn't look up but kept her eyes firmly fixed on her own feet. The darkness gave way to bright star shine. Mostly the stellar sparkles appeared as white light, but within the brightness, all colours of the spectrum were present, including turquoise, but to no greater or lesser extent than any other colours. She could see that now. She continued to focus on the darkness beneath her. Nothing moved. Nothing appeared. Holly's feet touched the unseen solidity of the library floor. The clear summer morning light of the library's internal illumination kicked in and a dry, rustling voice at the back of her head said, "Welcome back. We missed you."

Holly held her ground, "Hello to you too, but I probably should ask, albeit somewhat after the event, who or what, precisely, are you? Also, and I don't mean to presume your answer or be picky, but if you are what I think you are, aren't you with me all the time? What's with all the 'welcome back' thing?"

There was further rustling, then the voice said, "You knew us. You know us. We are here, and we have been with you ever since you opened up to us. We are the thoughts and knowledge dwelling within this library, built up, slowly and unstoppably over time. We are words within books and the thoughts of people as they read them. We are the words readers whisper to one another to communicate their thoughts. We are gathered together and held together by the magics within the library. You freed us and then added your own experiences to our collection. The memories you brought with you and then made here augmented us. We are of the library, and in the library, and within the part of the library that now resides inside you. We are in you and surrounding you. You are inside us and surrounding us and are a part of us. We are always here and always with you. We are stronger now, because we are all once again co-located within the same mother source. You are now home. We are again home, but we were always here. Is that a sufficiently complete answer?"

"Yes," said Holly slowly, whilst producing a lightweight pine chair with an unnecessary wave of her hand so she could sit while she mulled over what had just been said. The voice in her head waited patiently, providing just a faint rustling as a backdrop to her thoughts. Eventually, Holly spoke again, "And Partridge? I saw him here yesterday. What was that about? Did you have anything to do with his appearance?"

"We are always here and always with you. We became stronger then, and again now, because we are all returned to the source. We were focused and together, but nothing that was not part of us was present. Your memories are always part of us."

"So you're saying I just imagined seeing Partridge yesterday? He was simply my memory playing tricks?"

"We are not saying that. We do not know, but," and here the voice changed subtly, becoming less dry, "your memories are part of our connection. They flow through it and enhance it. We resonate to you. You were the only physical presence here, yesterday, girlie. It's for you to go figure out what took place and what you actually saw."

"Partridge? Is that you?"

"Yes and no. I'm a memory of myself. Whenever I visited the library, I left traces behind me. We all do. But then, on my final visit, I believe I left more than a slight trace. I'm also inside your memories. Combine all that with your connection to the library," the voice sank back into dryness, "and I can be brought to the surface like water on top of a sea wave, but I remain part of the ocean." The voice briefly became Partridge's once more, "Had you thought about it logically yesterday, rather than panicking like a headless hen, you'd have worked it out for yourself, Holly girl. You're far too emotional for your own good. But, then again, you're not as ignorant as you look, so I guess, maybe, there's hope."

Holly's hackles rose as they always did when Partridge treated her like a child, but this time round, her brief flash of well-worn anger felt somehow comforting and then sad, like an old loved coat that finally had to be thrown away because it had become too worn to wear. It was the sadness that won, and Holly burst into tears.

"Holly girl, you're not crying again, are you? Soggy tears and old book paper do not make for a good combination. The books are uncomfortable. We would like you to stop crying."

Whether it was the familiar tones of Partridge or the reminder that this Partridge was not wholly himself, Holly wasn't clear. In any event, Holly produced a box of man-size tissues, wiped her eyes, blew her nose, and reclaimed her composure.

"Okay. I'm good. Things got the better of me for a moment, but I'm good, really I am." There was an extended silence with, perhaps, just the slightest of rustlings to indicate there were still listeners. "So, what do we do now?"

It was Partridge's voice that answered. "I rather thought you'd got some cataloguing work to do, girlie. These books aren't going to organise themselves." Pause. "Well, maybe some of them could, but overall they need your assistance. I'd get stuck in, if I were you. If you're going to do it properly, it's going to take a very long time, and I do recommend that you do it properly. You never know what you might find." There was a further extended silence. Holly waited, but there were no more sounds of any description.

Holly turned with a view to organising herself and her surroundings for the onerous cataloguing task ahead and then she felt a presence, a distinct feeling she was no longer alone in the library. She swung back round. There was no one there, but she still felt she was being watched. In the back of her skull, she heard the faintest of whispers. Partridge again.

"Plus, you've yet to work out how you saw me when I really wasn't there."

CHAPTER 14

Cataloguing the Coven's old and extensive library was an immensely time-consuming project, requiring a logical, methodical approach, commitment, perseverance, and stamina. Holly forced herself to knuckle down to the task, and the library's voices left her to it. She was both grateful and upset by this. She valued the uninterrupted quiet but felt very strongly that matters had been left floating in the air by Partridge's parting comment. If truth be told, she also missed Partridge's audible presence, even if she knew it was a fake one.

Several long days into the task, Holly came to the conclusion that cataloguing the books "properly" without using magic at all was not viable. She calculated it would take several lifetimes to complete the task the mundane way and that was lifetimes that had been extended significantly by Old Magic. Cataloguing by magic alone was obviously doable, but would result in Holly "knowing" everything without knowing precisely what she knew, until some thing, event, or need brought the information to the surface. She was worried that key information could easily get lost in the ocean of facts and opinions absorbed and this, she thought, could undermine her aim of really learning about the Coven and the recent visual anomaly, for want of a better term, in the library. Holly therefore settled on a combination of magic and mundane manual labour. Things were still going to take a long time, but at least she could look forward to sifting consciously through the information available to her within a period of months as opposed to decades.

As planned, Holly made the work a nine-to-five operation, working on days when Jake was on duty and allowing herself the opportunity to work on beyond five when her witchlight alarms or a simple mobile phone call told her that Jake was working late himself. She made sure she was always back at Basingfield Lane a few minutes before Jake, with the dinner apparently prepared the traditional, non-magic way on the grounds that it would keep Jake happy, and a little white deception never hurt anyone. Except, she was becoming increasingly concerned that she was now intentionally deceiving Jake on a regular basis and he clearly needed the deception to be happening. She was also extremely uncomfortable about the "little woman home for her man with tea already on the table" role that she somehow seemed to have slipped into. For the time being, though, she justified it to herself on the grounds that she was the one with the time, capability, and magic to create a harmonious domesticity of readily available, healthily cooked meals.

The one and only time she had persuaded Jake to take responsibility for the evening meal, he had been delayed by a difficult bovine breach birth and had arrived home late, tired, and filthy and incapable of preparing anything more than beans on toast. Even then, Holly had had to assist.

"Holly, darling, I've got to get showered and changed. Would you mind cutting the bread and putting the toast on? I'll do the beans when I come back down."

Half an hour later, the toast was cold and Jake still wasn't down. When Holly went upstairs to see what was happening, she discovered Jake fast asleep on the bed wrapped only in a soggy towel. She magicked up a plateful of hot beans on fresh toast and a steaming mug of tea that she brought up to him.

All in all, Jake seemed content with the domestic routine they had wrapped themselves in, and, on the surface, their relationship was comfortable, settled, and loving, but there were the ongoing deceptions, Holly's increasing disquiet at her assumed "little domestic woman" role, and the fact that Jake never, ever asked her how her day had been beyond a rather perfunctory,

"Another hard day at the library, eh love? They'll be making you Head Librarian if you're not careful." He didn't seem to want to know the details of the project or what her individual days involved, and Holly didn't tell him.

Despite her newfound industry — or perhaps because of it — Holly was careful to maintain the routine of her weekly lunch date with Sarah. It was always fun and gave her an outlet for her concerns about the situation with Jake, as well as a chance to talk through her experiences at the library. Though, as Holly had kept Sarah in the dark about her witchlight, and Sarah wasn't really that interested in old books, their chats had their limitations.

"Another hard week at the library, eh Holly? You'll be Head Librarian in no time, though why you want to go and do quite so much voluntary work in a library when you're rolling in it is beyond me. What's the current Librarian like? Male? Good looking? I could see the attraction in working for a fine specimen of manhood…"

Holly shrugged. "I've never actually met him. I just deal with the receptionists. And even then it's little more than a "hello, good morning, and good night, have a nice evening," sort of relationship."

Sarah sipped her chilled white wine,

"So, what are the receptionists like? Any hot male eye-candy available?"

"For a married woman, you are incorrigible. Jemima and Mary are both lovely… ladies. Marcus is male, fit, toned, and with the most gorgeous ebony skin, but he's strictly a guy who likes guys. Finton is also male and not bad looking for a man who won't be seeing sixty-five ever again, but he's a bit too old for me." Holly left out the constant accompanying presences of the four witches' familiars: Jemima's Cyril, Fred the Great Dane, who occupied more of the area behind the reception desk than Mary did, the miniature schnauzer who was always at Marcus's heels, and Petrus, the white rabbit who lived in Finton's jacket pocket. She also didn't let on that Finton would not be seeing sixty-five again because he was already ninety-three, but looked about forty-three and was, Holly admitted to herself, quite cute with it in a bookish sort of way. It was amazing what a dab or three of witchlight could achieve.

Holly's stated deprecation of Finton didn't put Sarah off. "Okay, so he's past retirement age, but he's still working, so there's life in the old dog yet. What's wrong with a book-loving silver fox? You'll be turning forty next month, so what's twenty-five years here or there?"

"Sarah, really! I've got Jake. We love one another. I'm not going to be off hunting silver-foxes, thank you very much."

Sarah grasped the conversational thread and re-directed it.

"Yes, and you need to hang on to Jake Wortham. He's one of the good guys and a looker, to boot. Your track record with men is hardly inspiring, and you need to keep pulling out all the stops for this one. Still, it's no bad thing to have Mr. Librarian lined up alongside in case things do go pear-shaped."

"That's not nice and anyway, there were good reasons why all those old relationships ran off the rails. It's not going to happen this time to Jake and me. We're… good."

Sarah sensed Holly's hesitation and launched into another tirade about sweet-keeping Jake while staying on the hunt for other possibilities, which did little or nothing to help Holly untangle or tackle the issues that were accumulating round her and Jake.

Despite Sarah's regular pep-talks, the issues just continued to accumulate. Holly and Jake didn't encourage them, but they did nothing meaningful about tackling them, either. Holly's now-established routine continued to flow onwards routinely, and nothing much seemed to progress except the number of books that Holly was steadily cataloguing for the library.

Holly was finding the books interesting, but she hadn't really learned anything new to her except a neat trick involving a brick wall and a forest of butterflies as a way to confound pursuing enemies. She quite fancied trying it out sometime, despite the fact that she didn't really have any enemies these days that she was aware of. Except, of course, there was the Coven — but she was hoping things had improved there.

The Coven was being quiet and amenable and was letting her get on with the library work. She hadn't seen Caprice Graham since the project had begun, and on the one occasion she had contacted Caprice with an offer to update her on progress, she had received a brisk, "Thank you, Sister Beldam, but as fascinating as the Coven's antiquarian books undoubtedly are, I'll have to pass at the moment. Busy, busy, you understand."

Not for the first time, Holly wondered what had led the Coven to agree to the project in the first place.

There was also no further news about the disappearance (or discovery) of Brother James, and Holly concluded that the case had been closed. If this left matters hanging, she wasn't going to say so to anyone. She could live with not knowing what Brother James had been doing, presumably bunny-hopping around her house, or houses, if it meant that the hunting and eating habits of Barny and Grindlebones went uncommented on.

Based on the books in the library, and taking into account things written and not written, The Grand Coven of Great Britain, Ireland, and the Etheric Isles in their Domain was a dwindling power that was not so grand as it once was, or as it liked to think of itself as still being. Locked into ever-increasing self-imposed bureaucracy and historic delusions of power, the British Coven was no longer a power to be reckoned with. It curtailed the power of its witches rather than developed it, losing itself in arcane pomp and circumstance and a ceremonial masque of past glories, whilst allowing witchery to decline. It was probably the reason Ninanna had got away with her dark practices for so long. If she hadn't, in effect, created her own nemesis in the form of Holly's dazzling witchlight, she would be the one with real power and might even now be the black, calf leather gloved hand controlling a puppet Coven. Though, Holly felt her grandmother's preference would have leaned towards ignoring the constrained pettiness of the Coven and remaining a lone wolf unlimited by man-made borders.

As to where this left Holly in relation to things, Holly herself still did not know, so she got on with cataloguing and reading selected books, while mentally preparing the next evening meal for Jake and herself.

Days drifted into weeks, into a month and more, possibly even longer, technically speaking. Holly had started to bend time to increase her progress through the book stock and still be back home in time for supper with Jake.

There was no word from the Coven or the rustling library consciousness and its simulacrum of Partridge. Partridge however, or another echo of him, had invaded Holly's dreams and was providing a sarcastic running commentary on the mind-numbing cataloguing work and the issues, personal and witchlight fuelled, that were troubling Holly's night time rest,

"Look here, girlie. I still don't understand why you don't just catalogue the whole damned library at one go. You've got the power to do it, you know. Like you did last time, only bigger and grander. Once you've got the information from the library, you could use Old Magic to catalogue it in a flash. Even basic magic interfaces with standard software these days. You could sort through the knowledge at your leisure. Witchlight is a better search engine than many I could mention but won't. They'll soon have an app for monitoring dreams, if they haven't already. You could have everything at your fingertips and time to spare.

"I don't mean to nag, but you still haven't worked out what caused you to see me, looking especially lovely, I might add, but that's not the point. My apparent corporeal return is. Yes, I was a particularly fine piece of man flesh, but... Now, there's no need to be getting prudish, young Holly. You know I was hot back in the day. Even your Chardonnay-swilling friend thought so. And on that note, I still don't understand why you haven't come out to her as a witch. Only broomsticks belong in the closet, believe you me. The woman's your best friend. Doesn't she deserve to know?

"Then again, you probably ought to sort out young Jakey boy first. Nice lad, all in all, but with an alarming aversion to magic, don't you think? That's probably not ideal given your witchlight pedigree and the strength of the light within you. Your heritage is truly special, whether you like it or not. You come from a long, long line of exceptionally powerful witches. You should honour them with both your witchlight and your physical body, not take up mundane clerical duties in a library or become a housewife. It's beneath you. You were born to be the final sacrifice..."

At this point in Holly's reoccurring dream, the twinkly Partridge inevitably began to transform into the black-draped Ninanna, and

Holly would wake up screaming. Jake was becoming quite used to it, and he was far from happy with the regular interruptions to his necessarily cherished sleep pattern. The working hours of a vet required him to get as much sleep as he could when he could.

"Holly, are you putting in too many hours with those damn books? Do you need to ease off a bit so we can both get some untroubled sleep? It seems like a good idea, eh? What do you think…? At which point, Jake usually succumbed to sleep once more, leaving Holly wide-eyed, awake, and fretful.

It was probably the lack of sleep — that even witchlight couldn't seem to address — which meant that Holly was not totally prepared for the book when she finally worked her way along the maze of dusty, untouched shelves to where it had been gathering the dust of ages to itself.

The book was old, but unexceptional looking, bound in faded tan leather. If anything, it seemed rather worn and uncared for compared to the books surrounding it. Its contents were something of a patchwork, apparently made up from pages culled from many different sources at different times, beginning with almost indecipherable hand-scrawled pages from sometime in the sixteenth century and ending in cheaply printed texts circa the 1950s. It had been annotated and scribbled on uncaringly by an assortment of different hands. Some of the earliest margin notes reminded Holly of Ninanna's spider scrawl, but she couldn't be really sure who the author was.

The most astounding thing about the book was the faded 1970s Polaroid wedged as an apparent afterthought into the back of the binding. Holly recognised it immediately. It was a photo of her at the age of nine standing outside the old St. Pancras station on the Euston Road.

She was so surprised by the photo that it took Holly a while to realise that what she was holding in her hands was, in effect, a book of prophecy.

CHAPTER 15

It was the photograph that concerned Holly the most for a whole variety of reasons including how, why, and who, but she also felt quite strongly that she needed to better understand the book she had found it in. Context seemed potentially important in this instance.

It was a book of prophecy, or rather, a book of prophecies, a patchwork collection of future gazing from different times and places. It was the only book of this type that Holly had so far come across in the Coven library. If she thought about it — and she was now doing so ten to the dozen — the lack of such manuscripts wasn't that surprising. You could do an amazing variety of things with witchlight and even more with raw or Old Magic, but predicting the future wasn't one of them. You could really only influence the here and now of things. Sure, you could bend time a little, but that was working with the laws of physics and only affected time as you were immediately experiencing it. There was no way a witch could look at what hadn't happened yet. Holly was sure of it. Well, almost sure. She had absorbed all the Coven's lore of and information about Old Magic during her painful confrontation with Ninanna, and there was nothing in it or her own experiences to make her believe different. Still, Holly always preferred to be safe rather than sorry. She decided to throw caution away on her witchlight and check what else might be lurking in the library on the subject of seeing into the future. Of course, this wasn't strictly in keeping with her signed agreement with the Coven, but needs must, she thought.

Holly paused in her perusal of the book. She stood motionless, closed her eyes, and forced her body to relax. She imagined her body slowly pushing out tentacles of witchlight, probing feelers of pure white light that were stretching away from her in search of information connected to the act of prophecy. Her imagination became real, and in an increasing flood of brightness, the witchlight poured out and away from her, seeking, and ultimately absorbing information from the great library.

Wondering how long the process was going to take, Holly braced herself for the light's return. The last time she had harvested information in this way in this particular location, it had returned to her in wave after wave of light that became an almost unbearable flood. This time, she was ready for it. She was also trying to keep things practical and had consciously envisaged the returning light splitting into two: one stream bearing the information she was seeking back to her, the other uploading book information into the catalogue database. Well, Holly thought, there was no point in wasting the effort. Besides, it would cut down on the mundane activity required to complete the cataloguing task.

Holly continued to wait. Things seemed to be taking longer this time. She started to worry. Was there going to be too much information to deal with? The last time had opened her up to the library. Would an even greater payload of information expose her even further? Was this a really wise thing to be doing without much forethought? And then her witchlight returned, or at least she thought it did.

There was a single pulse of power, a brief and basically rather feeble spurt of light, and the computer containing the database chirruped half-heartedly. And that was that.

Holly opened her eyes and peered into the once-more gloomy distance. Could she make out any more light on its way back to her? No. So that truly was that. What exactly did she now know that she didn't know before?

Holly searched inside herself. The inability of even Old Magic to look into the future was a belief held by just about the whole of witchery. The exceptions were few and far between and usually somewhat mentally uncertain. One old woman back in the sixteenth century had claimed she could see into the future, and the Coven had

had her burnt at the stake via the unwitting intermediary services of a church purge. And that seemed to be about it. Really?

Then, from the back of Holly's skull, a dry voice that echoed ever so slightly with Partridge's droll intonation whispered, "Samuel Lighthowlers."

"Sorry, what?" Holly found herself snapping at the surrounding emptiness.

"Samuel Lighthowlers." This time it was Partridge's slightly annoyed and clearly enunciated tones that Holly heard. Possibly over enunciated. Holly felt that Partridge was making a point.

Holly considered the name. From a memory she didn't know she had, and probably hadn't until two minutes previously, she dredged up, "Samuel Lighthowlers, born circa 1500, date of death unknown — 'My dreamth do illuminate the darkness of the yeares ahead. I see a harvesting of the old magicks into a single receptacle that will wield mighty powere over everything that liveth and breetheth and also over those that have formerly donne so.'

"These lines, and a few other inconsequential and basically non-sensical jottings, appear in Lighthowlers' diary. Whilst taken seriously by a few Old Magic practitioners at the time, nothing more came of it, and the 'prophecy' was soon forgotten."

The fact that the remembered text referred to jottings in a diary made Holly pause. She re-read, or attempted to, the almost indecipherable handwritten pages at the beginning of the found prophecy book. Now she knew what she was looking at and what the text might mean, she recognised the words of Samuel Lighthowlers. Given the content of the text, the spider scribble in the margins suddenly took on greater significance.

"Wytchlyte floweth in the bloode. Capture the bloode, trappe the lyte" and *"Wytchlyte floweth between he who leadeth the family and he who endeth it."*

And then in a more modern script, but a very similar hand, *"Head of the family, end of the line."*

The more Holly looked at the more modern writing, the more it reminded her of Ninanna's scrawl. There were other notes and annotations in the same hand, and they all echoed the ways in which

Ninanna had accumulated and harvested the witchlight of their family. Other notes in a different writing style appeared to mirror the first set.

Was this what had set Ninanna off on her deadly rampage through her own family, or was Holly just reading things into the antique manuscript that weren't really there?

Holly swiftly leafed through the later pages of the prophecy book. Now she suspected what she was looking at, it was clear that most of the sections were basically about the same thing — the process of gathering and increasing witchlight via Old Magic practices and predictions, or more appropriately, suppositions, that somebody would actually do this, *was* doing it (according to some of the marginalia). Much of it was incomprehensible, "*Circle rounde eleven, Twelfth the circle rounde*" whatever that meant, for example, but the point was that others had found meaning in it.

Holly was as convinced as she could be that Ninanna had seen and read this book and had made some of the handwritten notes in it. She had no idea, however, who had made the other notes. She also couldn't work out why, given that the book was about Old Magic, she hadn't found it the previous year when she had, in effect, ransacked the archive for every drop of information about Old Magic. Then there was the really big, still unanswered question: What was an old Polaroid of Holly doing within the covers of the book?

Holly stared at the photo. She could remember quite clearly when it had been taken. There had been a day trip to Central London with her adopted mother. They had caught the train from East Croydon Station to Victoria and from there had taken The Tube to Trafalgar Square to see Nelson's Column and feed the pigeons. In the square, they had bought a little bag of bird seed, and Holly had spent a happy time with the pigeons perching on her and eating seed from her outstretched hands. It had been such fun, and her mother never even commented on the pigeon poo. She had simply cleaned her up. They had eaten their sandwiches in the square and had then done some window shopping before going back home. But — and Holly couldn't remember why — they had gone out of their way to visit St Pancras station. Holly had been so impressed by the Gothic grandness of the station and its hotel that she had asked Mum to take a photo of her as a keepsake. This was the photo.

She hadn't seen it for years. As far as she could remember, it had been kept in one of her mother's many photograph albums. They were presumably still at her parents' house down in Croydon, though only her father lived there now, and he was on an extended visit to his sister in Canada. He was, however, bound to know where they were. As much as she wanted to, and technically could, Holly couldn't just turn up in the middle of Canada and say, "Hi, Dad, how are you doing? Do you remember where you've put Mum's old photograph albums?" She could, though, transport herself down to Croydon while he was away and search for the albums herself.

Normally, Holly would have magicked herself down to South London directly from the library, but there was only one way in and one way out of the lower archive and that was via the Pentagram. She'd have to leave her work and go to the upper area before transporting. So, she decided to carry on with her cataloguing work and go to Croydon when she had finished at the library for the day.

Holly attempted to settle her mind back into the routine of checking and recording books, but the ragtag book of prophecy kept weighing on her mind and the photograph even more so. What was it doing in the book? Had Ninanna stolen it once she was aware of Holly's identity? If so, why? Or could the photo have ended up in the book some other way? The possibility of Ninanna's involvement in matters currently connected to the library made Holly exceptionally uncomfortable.

Holly wasn't really concentrating on the task in hand and after double entering a book on Swedish antique mirrors — and why that was in the Coven's collection was anybody's guess — she decided to call it a day somewhat earlier than usual.

Marcus and Friedrich the schnauzer had been on duty when Holly arrived that morning. They were still sitting at the reception desk when Holly emerged from the book stacks two hours earlier than usual. Marcus was engrossed in a vast Dostoevsky novel, and Friedrich was paying attention to a doggy chew that had, apparently, already seen much doggy attention. It was obviously a quiet day.

"Hi Marcus. I'm off a bit early today. I've got some errands to run."

"Sure thing, Holly. No worries." Marcus grinned, but didn't take his eyes away from the book he was reading. Friedrich, however, stopped gnawing at his chew, cocked his ears, and looked (to Holly's eyes) somewhat questioning. "What's up, boy?" Marcus scratched his familiar's ears, and Friedrich gave a little shudder of pleasure before resuming his assault on the chew. Holly took this as her cue to depart.

"I'll be off, then. I'll be back tomorrow at the usual time. Strong light," and she walked briskly through the front wall and into the empty lift shaft before either Marcus or Friedrich could look up again.

Once she had risen up the shaft and emerged in the mundane British Library, Holly wandered away from the crowds and found a gloomy corner she could literally disappear into and then transport herself across London to her father's empty, terraced house.

Holly materialised in the lounge. It was quiet and a bit dusty and looked as it had always looked, homely and comfortable. The furniture had been new back in the 1960s, but now it was old and somewhat tired in appearance, but it also had the emotional patina of things that had been well loved.

Holly went straight to where she assumed the photograph album would be, the old-fashioned, glass-fronted bookcase in one corner of the room. Both her parents had been creatures of habit, and since her mother had died last year, her father had stuck to their tried and tested ways of doing things.

The albums were in the bookcase as expected. They were mock-leather bound and looked as well-loved and dated as the bookcase that surrounded them. Holly took them out of the bookcase and sorted through them. Her memory said there should be seven, but she could only see six. The photographs and albums had been arranged chronologically, and it was the album containing the first photos of her, from the time she was adopted as a baby up until her tenth birthday, that was missing.

Holly looked round the room but couldn't see the absent album. Standing up, she took two paces into the uncluttered middle of the room, visualised the missing album, and willed it to emerge from wherever in the house it had been placed. She extended her hands, palms upwards, expecting the album to drop into them. It didn't. She willed the album to appear again, but once more, it declined to oblige or could not. Holly hadn't expected this.

Using Old Magic to tap into the ingrained essence of family present in the photo albums, Holly ran a tracer spell on the missing book. The first pass of the spell proved that the album was no longer in the house. Holly broadened the search area and repeated the spell. Nothing. She repeated the spell time and time again, each time broadening the scope of her search until she was covering most of the South East and Eastern England. Finally, her witchlight detected a faint presence in Cambridgeshire, less than a mile from Basingfield. Holly hadn't expected that, either.

Concentrating her witchlight on the area identified, Holly once more visualised the missing album and willed it to come to her. She extended her hands, palms upwards, and this time, the album appeared — or rather a sodden, water-stained, and mud-splashed brown paper parcel thudded and slightly squelched into her hands. One end of the package had been ripped or gnawed open, and the bedraggled remains of the photo album were sticking out of it. Holly was horrified by its sorry condition, but she couldn't afford to get upset at the state of what had been one of her mother's prized possessions. She needed to be calm and methodical in the way she approached things, or she might miss something.

First off, she studied the now almost indecipherable address on the outer wrapping. Fortunately, both the handwriting and the address were very familiar to her, which made working out where it had been posted to that much easier. The handwriting was her father's elderly scrawl. The address was her own. There were also some stamps and a postmark visible. The package had been posted just after New Year, a day or so before her father flew out to Canada. Come to think of it, at Christmas he had said there was something of her mother's he wanted her to have and he'd stick it in the post to her. Holly was a little upset that she'd forgotten all about it, but since the visit of Brother James in February, she had been somewhat distracted.

Holly's father had clearly remembered his promise and had posted the album shortly after telling her he would, but it had never arrived. Judging from the location she had retrieved it from and its all too sorry state, the package had been received or intercepted by someone else, opened, and then dumped in a ditch between the Cambridgeshire villages of Basingfield and Meldran. But why and by whom? If it had been delivered in the area, but to the wrong address, wouldn't someone have at least returned it to the sender's address or possibly have got the Royal Mail to re-deliver it, given the likely proximity to the intended addressee?

Holly needed to check out the album itself to see if anything had been done to it, but it was too wet and damaged to open without ruining it further. She was scared of destroying the irreplaceable photos.

Holly focused and once again willed and directed her witchlight. There was a faint flash of white light, and the album and its contents were restored to their original state. If anything, they now looked in better repair than the sibling albums. Holly, had, however, been careful to restore the album as it actually was and not make any changes to whatever may have been done to it by the person or persons unknown who had opened her parcel without her say so.

With some trepidation, she opened the photograph album and examined the contents. Everything was as she had expected to see it, except for one blank space where a photograph had clearly been removed. Judging from the remaining photographs around the gap, it was the instant photo of Holly outside St. Pancras station. As to why this photo was absent, there was no indication. Nor were there any visible or magical traces of the person who had removed it.

Holly was not prepared to be defeated. If magic alone could not provide an answer, perhaps magic combined with mundane sleuthing could.

Holly focused on the stained and unrestored brown paper wrapping. From its unpromising surface, a range of previously invisible fingerprints appeared. Holly enhanced them and using wholly magical and less than legal means, searched UK police databases for a match. Most of the prints did not match any records, although it appeared that there was a Royal Mail operative down in South London who'd had a bit of a colourful past in his day. There were other prints on top of his, so Holly didn't think he was the person responsible for the misdirection of her package.

Following a hunch, Holly transported herself and the album back to Basingfield Lane and checked for fingerprints at the property. Despite her command of powerful magic, Holly was not a totally scrupulous house cleaner, and images of prints located around the house soon started appearing. Holly made a mental note to be more thorough with the cleaning magics in future, whilst being grateful that so far she hadn't been.

Holly arranged the found prints in the air in front of her, like they did in high tech police procedurals, although they usually had some form of glass screen to project the images on to. Holly was just using the air in her lounge. She quickly eliminated her own prints and those of Jake. Whilst, in addition, there were plenty of paw prints, especially muddy ones, there were relatively few prints left by humans, just Sarah, Mark, and a handful of other friends. None of them matched those on the parcel.

With a sigh of resignation, Holly transported herself, the album, and its wrapping to the cottage in Oxfordshire where she repeated the fingerprint searching process. As before, she eliminated her own prints and those of Jake, although there were far fewer of the latter here than at Basingfield Lane. She searched through the remaining unidentified prints until she found a set that matched the ones taken from the parcel. They had come from the lounge wall where a heavily perspiring Brother James had put out his hand to steady himself when he had almost trodden on Barny. It would appear that Brother James had been the person who had ripped open Holly's mis-appropriated parcel.

CHAPTER 16

Holly was now back at Basingfield Lane but was still contemplating the many possible implications of Brother James' fingerprints when Jake arrived home. His somewhat resigned, "What's up now?" was the first indicator that perhaps Holly had been mulling over things for a bit too long: too long for her own peace of mind and too long to pretend she had prepared the evening meal the old-fashioned, mundane way.

Holly took a deep breath and possibly a little too quickly said,

"I'll just magic up dinner for us and then I'll explain. What would you like to eat? Anything at all. You choose."

Jake's somewhat begrudging, "Simple steak and chips, as light on the magic as possible, would suit me fine, but I'll need to get cleaned up first," was an unneeded indicator that all was once again not right in their domestic world. Other than her unthinking offer to magic up dinner, Holly couldn't work out why.

Holly waited for Jake to shower, and once she could hear him on his way back downstairs, she made as undramatic a gesture as possible towards the kitchen table. In theory, she didn't need to gesture at all, but in moments of stress, she still found it difficult not to, and, actually, also in moments of non-stress. Despite the raw power she possessed, she was still finding her way through various beginner witches' quirks. Notwithstanding the unnecessary finger pointing, the table was immediately laid and two plates of piping hot steak, chips, and peas, with crispy onion rings on the side, appeared along with a bottle of vintage red wine and two wine glasses already filled with the tempting Shiraz. The combined aromas were making Holly's mouth water, and she had created them.

Jake walked slowly into the kitchen, grunted his thanks (at least Holly assumed it was thanks), sat down at the table, and started to eat.

Holly sat down opposite him.

"How is it?"

"Lovely."

"It's okay then?"

"Succulent steak. Perfectly cooked golden chips. Onion rings dry and crispy, just how I like them. Couldn't be better. Then again, with your magic, it never can be better. Your dinners are always the pinnacle of perfection, even the ones you tell me you have cooked the old-fashioned way using an oven and assorted traditional kitchen utensils." Jake shovelled another forkful of perfectly cooked steak into his mouth.

"And that's bad because?"

"Didn't say it was bad, just invariably perfect."

"Uh huh?"

The only sounds in the kitchen were the subdued ticking of the kitchen wall clock and Jake slowly chewing on his steak. Though it was so tender it didn't really require that much mastication.

Holly started on her own dinner. Half way through the undoubtedly wonderfully cooked and very quiet meal, Holly decided to tell Jake about her discovery of the Polaroid photograph and the revelation, in the fullest sense of the word, that Brother James had apparently intercepted a package sent to her at Basingfield Lane by her father and opened it.

"A revelation? Really? That's a bit over the top even by the dramatic standards of witchcraft."

"It was revealed. I revealed it, and it reveals further issues, namely that Brother James was more snuckilly sneaky than he let on. He was clearly up to more than he had told me about. The question is why and who else was involved? If others had something to do with it, maybe it wasn't Barny and Grindlebones who murdered him?"

"What?" Jake spat out the chips he had been chewing. "Murdered?"

"Yes, you know. We talked about it a couple of months ago. If you remember, I said the boys might have 'partaken' of rabbit Brother James."

"Eaten, you mean. You might have said that, but there was no mention of murder."

"But we talked about it. I said the cats might have, probably, almost certainly killed a rabbit, the big one they brought into the house and were fighting over. Only the rabbit was most likely Brother James. Wholly natural for cats, but a very unfortunate for Brother James. Of course," Holly added hopefully, "that particular rabbit might not have been Brother James. The boys may just have found his corpse after its demise at someone or something else's hand or paw. They may not have carried out the actual ki…"

"Murder. It would have been murder. You just said so, and you've never mentioned murder before."

"Well, I don't think it was actually murder and you don't too, but I'm not sure about what the Coven would make of it."

"Speak for yourself, not for me, please."

"Oh?"

"Yeah."

"Yeah, what?"

"Well, let's think about that, shall we? You may be a super powerful witch. You may automatically achieve perfection with a waggle of your little finger. You may be harbouring a pair of homicidal cats. But you don't, shouldn't, can't speak for me."

"I didn't mean…"

Jake interrupted, "No, you never mean, but it still happens."

"What, exactly, happens?"

"Death. Dead people. Dead witches. Homicidal animals. Bad magic. Take your pick. They surround you like flies around a horse."

"Jake, please…"

"No. No more, please. I have tried, Holly. I really have, but I just can't cope with any more of this. Your grandmother tried to rip my guts out with her huge bloody dog. Dogs are bred to hunt. Was that wholly natural too? Since then, you've wrapped me up in cotton wool so tight I can hardly breath. *I'll look after you. I'll cook for you. I'll take you away on yet another holiday.* Everything is perfect. Everything is just so, particularly when once again you are using magic at the drop of a hat for even the smallest domestic things. But 'perfection is insipid in the naughty world of ours,' and now your cats are 'naturally' re-enacting slasher films in the back field. I can't cope with it anymore. I won't cope with it. I need to get back to normal. To cows and cow shit and simple, reliable science. Back to where the world is how I've always understood it."

"That's not fair. A lot of what you've said isn't true. Where is all this coming from? Why now and what's with the 'perfection is insipid' thing?"

"It's Byron. I like Byron. I used to read a lot of Byron, but it doesn't surprise me that you don't know this. You're too wrapped up in your Old Magic and this witchlight malarkey to pay much attention to what I like or don't like, except in the bedroom and that's no doubt as much about your pleasure as it is for mine."

"It's not witchlight malarkey. It's magic. It's power. It's who I am. And yes, I like sex, but specifically, I like sex with you, because you're hot and good in bed, and because I love you. It's all because I love you."

"And, God help me, I love you too, but I can't take this any more. I thought I could adjust and that our love would be strong enough, but it isn't. I'm not. I'm still stretched out all the way to snapping, and I can't go through another evening like this, pretending everything is fine when it clearly isn't. You may be fine with your murderous, furry little darlings, but I had to deal with your grandmother's beloved four-footed best friend trying to grab a meal of liver and kidneys: mine. I need to get back to who I was. To go home, my old home. I haven't sold it yet. The last buyer fell through, so it's still there and that's where I'm going to go. I'm sorry, Holly. I really am, but I can't do this anymore. I need life to be simple again. Normal. Just… normal."

Jake threw down his knife and fork, shoved back his chair, and stood up. It took no more than a few steps across the kitchen to pick up his coat and car keys, then he strode down the hallway to the front door.

"Magic all my stuff over, why don't you. I'm sure it'll be easy enough for you to do." And with that, he opened the front door, walked through it, and slammed it shut.

Holly was left sitting in the echoing silence of her now-empty kitchen. She was dimly aware of a faint click as the cat flap swung shut behind a set of rapidly departing feline paws, closely followed by a second set. Even the occasional rustling at the back of her head chose this time to be silent.

CHAPTER 17

Holly hadn't had much sleep. Thoughts had been racing through her head all night. None of them pleasant. She'd sensed that things were uncomfortable between her and Jake, but not *that* uncomfortable. Not potentially terminal. What had happened? What could she have done, should she have done, to prevent this? How could she get things back on an even keel? Could she use Old Magic to get him back, or would that just make things worse?

She had finally dozed off and fallen into a dream where she had magicked Jake back to her, only to turn him inadvertently into a pink and grey cat who Barny and Grindlebones kept picking on. Each catfight, Jake came off worse, and now he was lying in her bed, bleeding and bedraggled, except he currently looked more like a rabbit than a cat, and the two boys were waiting outside the bedroom door for him to emerge. They started scratching and banging to be let in. She woke up with a start to find that the other half of her bed was cold and empty. Jake really had left her.

Holly stretched across the empty bed towards her bedside table, held out her hand and her mobile phone appeared in it, already dialling Jake's number. It rang, but he didn't answer. She rang again and a third time, but all she heard each time was, "Hello, you've reached the answerphone of Jake Wortham. Please leave your name and number and I'll get back to you. If it's an urgent issue requiring a vet, please ring the practice on…." If she hadn't known it already, she could have recited the surgery number from memory by the end of the third call.

Holly lay back down and managed to doze off again for an hour or maybe just a few minutes. She didn't know which and didn't check the time, just reached for her phone and tried calling Jake again and again with exactly the same results.

The light through her drawn bedroom curtains started to lighten ever so slightly as dawn sluggishly began to glimmer into day. Holly hadn't heard footsteps or a car engine but suddenly, there was a loud knocking on the front door.

Holly's green silk dressing gown immediately appeared around her, and she was rushing downstairs to throw open the door, but it wasn't Jake. Standing on her doorstep was a grey-suited Brother Wainthorpe, accompanied by Brother Lincoln, also in the ubiquitous grey suit, and a tall, unknown man in a black, hooded, ankle-length robe. Given the amazingly inappropriate medieval garb, Holly assumed he was a Coven Elder whom she hadn't previously met.

"Good morning, Sister Beldam. It is almost morning, I believe. May we come in?" It was the robed man who spoke. His voice was deep, slow, and accentless.

Holly was badly wrong-footed. Firstly, the incongruous trio outside her front door were not Jake. Secondly, they were not Jake. And finally, they were not Jake. In between, Holly was conscious that three Coven officials were now outside her mundane Cambridgeshire home, and one was prepared to be seen in public looking like something from the Medieval Grand Inquisition. Up until now, she had never seen witches try to look anything but contemporary in public, whatever they might choose to wear in the privacy of Coven gatherings.

Temporal dissonance aside, Holly realised she needed to take control of this situation — or as much control as she could manage given the circumstances.

"No, gentlemen. I do not wish to seem unduly rude, but I'm not prepared to invite you into what is basically a mundane home. My partner," Holly hesitated for a second, but struggled on, "is not a witch, and I try to keep this house as clear of magic and witchcraft as possible. If you wish, you may accompany me to my official address, as formally registered with the Coven. I am, I must admit, more than a little perturbed that you have chosen to call here and not there in the first place."

"Indeed, Sister Beldam." It was the black robed man who was once again talking, "But I am afraid we are here on a matter of some weight and could not afford to delay matters because of blind adherence to protocol."

"It must be important for a Coven Elder to be turning up in person at this time in the…" Holly peered towards the horizon, " pre-dawn and ignore protocol."

"I would assure you, Sister, it is."

There was a brief pause while Holly stared at her unwelcome visitors, and Brother Wainthorpe and the Elder stared right back. Brother Lincoln just looked like he would rather be anywhere else but where he currently found himself.

"So, gentlemen, will you accompany me to Oxfordshire?" Holly held out her hand expectantly. Brothers Wainthorpe and Lincoln somewhat reluctantly grasped it. The robed man merely nodded.

"Thank you, Sister Beldam, but I prefer to transport myself."

Holly responded by transporting herself and the two officials now physically connected to her from the front door of the Basingfield house to the garden path leading up to the front door of the black and white Oxfordshire cottage. As part of the process, Holly had made sure that she was wearing appropriate day wear of trainers, jeans, and a summer weight fawn jumper and no longer looked as if she had had a troubled and largely sleepless night.

About a second after the freshly attired Holly and her two escorts appeared in a slight puff of white light, there was an audible pop, and the be-robed Coven Elder appeared. Holly noticed that though his arrival produced sound, it was not accompanied by the usual splash of coloured witchlight.

He was clearly not happy to find himself once more outside one of Holly's properties. "I thought we were to accompany you inside, Sister Beldam?"

"Indeed, Brother? I've always understood that good manners require strangers to materialise outside a home prior to identifying themselves and being invited in. Brothers Wainthorpe and Lincoln I have, at least, met before. But with all due respect, I still do not know your name or your purpose."

Holly stared at the Elder, her head cocked slightly to one side. The silence was brief but noticeable.

"My name is Elder Nightingale. I am an Elder of The Grand Coven. These two Coven officials and myself are here to discuss the murder of Brother William James. Now, may we proceed?"

Holly's facial expression did not change, but the reference to the murder of Brother James made her tense inside. She had nothing to fear directly, but Barny and Grindlebones? She managed a faint smile,

"Well then, Elder Nightingale, Brothers Wainthorpe and Lincoln, please do go in." Holly pointed briefly to the heavy, solid oak front door of the cottage. It swung gently open.

Holly led the way through the door, down the white walled hallway and into the lounge, where she tactically positioned herself in the leather fireside chair before Elder Nightingale could get to it. Instead, he was obliged to perch himself somewhat incongruously on a small boudoir armchair upholstered in heavily floral fabric. Holly was about to offer everyone a cup of English Breakfast tea when Elder Nightingale peremptorily said,

"I think we can afford to dispense with trifling matters of etiquette. We are here to discuss the murder of Brother William James and your part in it."

Holly was taken aback by the directness of his speech and the implications of its accusatory tone, but she responded no less directly,

"Gentlemen, as saddened as I am by the untimely death of anyone, I must take exception to the accusation that I was in some way involved in Brother James's demise. As I have repeatedly told you — and as I am apparently going to have to do so again — the last I saw of Brother James was his retreating back as he exited via the self-same front door you have just come in by. He was very much alive at the time."

"Yes, so you say." It was Elder Nightingale again. "But, by your own admission, he was last seen here in Oxfordshire with you, and then elements of him turn up in the field behind your Cambridgeshire house. The link between these two disparate locations, Sister Beldam, is you and only you."

Holly's tone grew markedly frostier,

"I have gone over all of this before with Brothers Wainthorpe and Lincoln. I was not involved in his disappearance or death. I have no idea why he was in Basingfield, but I should very much like to know what he was doing there and why, apparently, he was intercepting my post."

Elder Nightingale's expression did not change. It was Brother Wainthorpe who snorted and said, "Post? Why would a witch bother with post? As for interfering with yours, this is the first I've heard of it."

Holly opened her mouth to respond, but Elder Nightingale was quicker,

"Hush now, Brother Wainthorpe. I'm sure all will become clear very shortly. This is just a further reason why we need to convene a Truth Council under the auspices of the Clerihorn. Don't you think?"

There was a smugness to his comment that Holly didn't like. She was also surprised at her unexpected feeling of revulsion at the mention of the Clerihorn. It was not as if she even knew what a Clerihorn was, so there was no point in getting upset about it. But then she realised she did know what a Clerihorn was. The information she had harvested from the library was waiting patiently to tell her. The unexplained feeling of revulsion gave way to an all too understandable sense of nausea.

"A Clerihorn? You have got to be joking. There hasn't been a Clerihorn for over 300 years, and even if there was a witch with all the requisite abilities, who in their right mind would want to resurrect such a medieval and basically barbaric process. You cannot be serious about this."

"You are mistaken, Sister Beldam. The last Clerihorn was conducted less than 100 years ago at a time of great need for both the Coven and the country. We feel we have need of the ritual again. A witch with your raw command of Old Magic would run circles around a standard Coven enquiry unless you are controlled in some way. Indeed, I suspect that you have been wilfully circuitous in your answers to the Coven for some time. So, I really think that a little order and control is now called for. That's all the Clerihorn is, you know: a short-term control mechanism for your witchlight, a temporary shackle for your power. Temporary, that is, unless you are found guilty."

Holly had grown pale from both anger and a growing sense of panic,

"It's more than a shackle. I know that, and you must too. It's a temporary torture until I am found guilty, or it all goes horribly wrong, which it has been known to do more than once. In which case, it's goodbye temporary. There is no way I'm going to agree to submit myself to such a thing."

By now, Nightingale was ignoring the other two Coven officials within the room. His focus was entirely directed on Holly,

"I must admit, I had anticipated your reluctance. That is why I have invited a certain someone to assist us in the process. It is a someone known to you whom you trust implicitly, which must be a reassurance, no? I am also assuming that it is someone you would not wish to see harmed in any way. If you would care to accompany us to the High Hall of the Coven, you will find Mister Jake Wortham is already there and waiting for you."

CHAPTER 18

I t was the same large, gloomily Gothic hall as before. The memory of her last meeting with a Coven gathering was unsettling enough in its own right. But now, after a sleepless night and with nothing to eat or drink since, there was the knowledge of what was to come. And, more worryingly, there was Jake.

Jake was seated on a large, heavy oak chair in the centre of the hall. He was not physically bound, but Holly could see the gun-metal grey witchlight draped around him, as effective as steel chains on a non-witch, and possibly on a witch, depending on how the magic had been put together. On the plus side (from Jake's point of view, though with mixed feelings from Holly's), the use of this particular magic meant that currently he was not aware of his situation or its implications. At least, Holly really hoped he wasn't. To all intents and purposes Jake was fast asleep, though sitting rigid and bolt upright on his restraining chair. His appearance— and indeed his presence — distressed Holly more than it distressed him, which gave Holly some strained comfort.

To the left of Jake, against a high stone pillar, was another chair. This one was made of blackthorn, living blackthorn, the aggressive, spikey thorns an integral part of the construction. Elder Nightingale gestured casually to the vicious seat as if it was a well-upholstered armchair. "Will you take your place, Sister Beldam?"

Holly hesitated. This was not going to be pleasant. Yes, she could use Old Magic to protect herself from the knife-like thorns, but the ensuing trial, or gratuitous torture — Holly hadn't quite made up her mind how best to define the Clerihorn — was designed to strip away her powers, leaving her vulnerable and exposed. The theory was that without the protection and dissembling of magic, the inner thoughts of the witch, and therefore the truth, would be revealed. Nothing in her head would be hidden from her interrogators, should they choose to look, including her concerns about Barny and Grindlebones and their role in the death and dismemberment of Brother James. Given their approach to humans, Holly didn't think the Coven would bat an eyelid about visiting "justice" on a pair of cats, however natural their behaviour had been.

Holly also knew from her bookish studies that the stripping away of a witch's protective magics had, in the past, resulted in the deaths of witches being investigated and, in extreme cases, others linked to the Clerihorn ritual. Others like Jake. It had started out as a medieval form of torture and its use had, supposedly, died out. But here it was being resurrected in the twenty-first century. Holly did not want to participate in it, but to refuse, even if she was physically able to do so — and she wasn't sure she was — would place Jake at even greater risk and immediately make her seem guilty in the eyes of the Coven.

Holly knew about the Clerihorn in theory, but the reality was quite a different thing. And she had no way of knowing whether her Old Magic, as strong as it was, would be powerful enough to enable her to refuse the ritual and save Jake or, indeed, survive the ritual unscathed. As evidenced by her last visit, it seemed she had badly underestimated the power the Coven could wield collectively. She could not afford to do that again. Not in these circumstances. Somehow, she had to find a way to get through the coming barbarities, protect Jake and herself, and shield Barny and Grindlebones from intolerant and unbending judgement.

Holly's thoughts had already started to run round her head like panicked lemmings in a maze, before it dawned on her that the intended process of the Clerihorn was already taking effect. Fear of the ritual was impeding her judgment, and therefore, the command of her power. She needed to clear her mind and focus if she was going to survive this intact. But then she caught sight of the witch who was taking on the role of the Clerihorn.

They were shrivelled and bent inwards on themselves like a caterpillar round a stick. She or he — Holly really couldn't tell which — was aged, wizened, and badly scarred. For a moment, Holly wondered why a witch would allow him or herself to appear like this when they could simply will themselves to look other, or, at the very least, disguise their appearance with a glamour. Then it dawned on her that the scarring was not just physical. The witch was mentally damaged too. There was a look of vacuity on the torn face that indicated the brain was as corrupted as the body that housed it. The only thing that appeared undamaged was the witchlight of the creature, but even that glowed pathetically dimly.

Elder Nightingale was still waiting and gesturing impatiently towards the blackthorn seat. He caught Holly's eye and then nodded towards the Clerihorn,

"Sister Saurua was the last person to be subject to the Clerihorn ritual. She failed the test, and then things did not go quite as they should. It happens sometimes, when so much power is being channelled and filtered. She has remained with us ever since, initially as punishment, but latterly in the hope that the next Clerihorn might generate enough power to restore her or set her free. Ninety odd years as a human vegetable, kept alive by the combined power of the Coven in case another Clerihorn could release her from her suffering. Think on that, Sister Beldam."

Holly felt physically sick at the thought of what the woman must have gone through and even more sick at the thought that, if things went wrong today, that could be her.

She was going to ask what, exactly, had happened to Sister Saurua to reduce her to this state, but Elder Nightingale gave her no time.

"We are waiting, Sister Beldam," he said, and the accompanying thin-lipped smile was not encouraging.

Holly looked again at the deformed and virtually powerless Clerihorn and then at Jake. She was scared, she admitted to herself. There were three Coven Elders in the hall besides Elder Nightingale, plus Brothers Lincoln and Wainthorpe, and the Clerihorn, though the latter's Witchlight was excessively weak. Holly wasn't even sure she would have the ability to perform the role. More worryingly, Holly was no longer sure that her own Old Magic fuelled witchlight was strong enough to take on so many. And even if she could, Jake was already covered in magic. She wouldn't be able to get him out easily. She needed to buy herself some time to think things through and find a way to control the process in order to do everything she could to make sure that things did not go the way of the last Clerihorn.

Holly made an effort to clear her mind and make a positive decision. Her anxious thoughts were determined to race, but somehow, she corralled them and forced them to work for her. Painfully, she arrived at some sort of a plan. She was going to undertake the trial, but on her terms, not the Coven's. What she was going to do was a big gamble, but if she had read the situation properly it might just work, and if it didn't, she could at least ensure that Jake stayed safe.

Holly walked slowly and hesitatingly towards the blackthorn chair, stumbling at least once. She looked almost as weakened as the Clerihorn, who had begun to shake, presumably from the strain of simply standing upright.

Watching her reluctant steps, Elder Nightingale smiled all the more broadly. As Holly reached the chair and slumped down onto the thorns of the seat with a defeated gesture, his smile grew broader still. When he noticed several deep scratches along her forearm and right thigh, he seemed to taste victory, and his witchlight burned brighter, finally revealing itself to be an icy blue. Holly's head slumped down onto her chest, and it looked as if she had lost the will to fight before the battle had even started.

Elder Nightingale was audibly pleased with himself, and his voice positively purred, "You are obviously aware of the ritual, Sister, but the tradition of the ritual itself demands I announce it loudly and clearly for all to hear." Elder Nightingale loosely indicated Jake, Brothers Lincoln and Wainthorpe, the Clerihorn, and the three nameless Elders — just enough of them to ensure that Coven protocols were seen to be adhered to. Then he smiled yet again. It appeared he just could not help himself. Had Holly been looking at him, she would have found the smile repellent, but her head remained slumped forward on her chest, her eyes closed.

"I therefore proclaim to all so gathered, that, there being three Elders present in addition to the Chief Inquisitor and two servants of the Coven, and there further being a person of light able to absorb the role of Clerihorn, a Truth Council is hereby convened to seek out the fate of Brother William James, loyal servant to the Coven, whose sad, deceased remains were potentially discovered in animal form in the County of Cambridgeshire, adjacent to the unregistered abode of Sister Holly Beldam. The truth of this Sister's involvement in the demise of Brother James will therefore be pursued by all means available, including the use of the Clerihorn, wheresoever it takes us. Are all those present agreeable for this to happen?"

No one said no, though no one present actually said yes, but Elder Nightingale wasted no time in moving on to the next stage of his announcement. He was obviously very keen for the process to commence.

"The Clerihorn will be the conduit of the truth. Sister Beldam will be allowed sufficient light to protect her physical being and that of the mundane male she has taken as a partner. That, and all other witchlight, will be channelled, shared, and absorbed by the chosen void that is the Clerihorn. The Clerihorn will consume as much witchlight as is needed to seek, find, and announce the truth. It may travel through the light into the mind of the witness to seek answers that are evasive. The Chief Inquisitor may add his own light to assist the process and focus power into any darkness that hides the truth until nothing remains hidden. Are all those present agreeable for this to happen?"

No one responded. As before, Elder Nightingale barely paused, before concluding,

"As the third and final sign of their agreement, I ask the three Elders here present to merge their light into a shield of protection around the trial arena so evil may not enter or leave and the truth shall remain protected."

The three Elders hesitated briefly and then raised their arms above their heads. As they lowered them, a field of combined witchlight surrounded Holly, Jake, the Clerihorn, and Elder Nightingale in a demisphere of translucent light that shimmered with multiple colours like a huge soap bubble. Elder Nightingale watched the shield descend with apparent fascination. The Clerihorn, Jake, and Holly all seemed oblivious to the magics surrounding them, although, in truth, Holly was all too aware of it.

"Sister Beldam." Elder Nightingale's tone of voice now had an edge to it. "Your attention, please. You may use sufficient magic to protect yourself from the blackthorn and to prevent this," a large and very weighty steel sword suddenly and unexpectedly appeared in the air above Jake, "from falling onto Mister Wortham. It is very sharp, so I recommend that you maintain focus, but you will need to do so via the Clerihorn. I acknowledge this is additional to the usual traditions of the Clerihorn ritual, but as your command of Old Magic appears unusually strong, it seemed a wise idea to make your shackles unusually arduous. Your witchlight must be poured, visibly, into the Clerihorn. I will monitor the flow to ensure its strength and purity.

"Once the flow has started, the Clerihorn will absorb as much of your witchlight as it needs to protect you and Mister Wortham as well as perform its own functions and seek the truth. It is badly damaged, and will no doubt require considerable light to play its part without faltering. But as you are an Old Magic practitioner, I'm assuming it won't be a problem for you. One last thing, I'm about to release my focus on the sword, so you need to focus your witchlight now."

The sharp sword above Jake's head wobbled for a brief moment, and then there was a blinding flash of white witchlight. Holly's head jerked upright, and a stream of light arced between Holly and the Clerihorn and from the Clerihorn to the sword. It did not falter. The Clerihorn opened its eyes. They blazed white and as brightly as Holly's witchlight. Its face and body glowed and were now transformed into those of a young woman with long, straight, pure-white hair, free of the scarring and extreme ageing that Holly had previously seen.

"I seek the truth," the Clerihorn intoned. "What would you know?"

"Did this witch kill Brother William James?" responded Elder Nightingale.

"No."

Nightingale clearly was not satisfied with the answer. "Are you sure? The answer was too swift. Even if she didn't kill him with her own hands, surely she was involved in his murder? Tell me the truth."

The Clerihorn now paused for what seemed like a long time and then spoke, "This witch had no hand in the death of Brother James. She is innocent of the crime. Seek into the nature of things for the cause of his death."

Elder Nightingale was visibly no longer happy. He glared at Holly and at the Clerihorn.

"What? Are you sure? Search again. There has to be a connection."

"I speak as I find. I find truth through power, and I speak truth to power. This witch did not murder Brother James."

Holly remained motionless. Her Witchlight continued to flow unabated into the Clerihorn. The sharp, heavy sword above Jake held steady. Ordinary witchlight would have been struggling by now, but Elder Nightingale did not seem concerned about the duress he was causing both Holly and the Clerihorn, or its potentially fatal effects.

"You've said that already, woman. I want to know if she was involved in some way. Any way whatsoever. I command you to respond."

The Clerihorn paused again, mulling over the words of Elder Nightingale and continuing to consume even more of Holly's witchlight while she did so. When she finally spoke, she was consistent in her response,

"I speak truth to power through power. The witch had no knowledge of his death until after the light had long since left him."

Nightingale was not giving up. While even more of Holly's power was drawn from her, he pondered and then slowly and precisely asked, "So, does she know who did it?"

Outside the bubble of shifting coloured light, the three Elders were becoming concerned. They had heard the answers from the Clerihorn and were satisfied with them. They knew how much witchlight was flowing from Holly to her, and they knew that anyone other than a user of Old Magic would be in serious trouble by now. What they didn't know was how much longer even Holly could keep going, or how long the Clerihorn itself could contain so much raw power.

Inside the bubble, Elder Nightingale had no such qualms,

"I asked and will know what knowledge this witch has of Brother James's death. Answer me."

This time, the Clerihorn's extended pause seemed to be more from exhaustion than a need to consider matters. The white fire in her eyes was beginning to dim. When she finally spoke, her words were slow and painfully drawn out, "Knowledge gained only after the event. I speak the truth I see. I have spoken truth. Now let me go."

Elder Nightingale did not appear to hear the final plea for humanity in the Clerihorn's pronouncement. "I refuse, I tell you, to accept she has no connection to Brother James' death. What is her link to his murder?"

The fire in the Clerihorn's eyes had all but disappeared, and the white glow that enveloped her was fading. Only the light supporting the lethal steel sword high above Jake remained unchanged. Outside the bubble, the three Elders had gone beyond concerned. They exchanged worried glances, and the bubble started to dissipate and melt downwards.

The Clerihorn half yelled, half whispered,

"This witch is not party to the murder of Brother James. Enough."

But Elder Nightingale continued to demand more. "I will have the truth. What links this woman to Brother James' death? Tell me, or I will probe her myself."

He strode toward the Clerihorn, his black robe flapping behind him, and seemed to be on the point of grabbing her by the throat. At this point, four things happened simultaneously: The encasing witchlight bubble disappeared completely; the sword suspended over Jake dropped half an inch and was then supported by three beams of multi-coloured light projected by the Elders; the Clerihorn screamed, and Holly pricked her thumb on a thorn. No one noticed that Elder Nightingale had apparently stopped in mid-lunge.

Holly's white witchlight rapidly began to fade from the Clerihorn. The woman screamed one more time, in a voice that was ageing even as she spoke, "I have spoken the truth. Nature was the cause and is the cause. I demand my own nature's rightful end. Let it be done." Her broken body slumped forward.

The Clerihorn was over.

CHAPTER 19

The three Elders now nominally in charge of the concluded Clerihorn were attempting to deal with three pressing matters: a dead Clerihorn, a furious Elder Nightingale, and an even more furious Holly. It was Holly they were rapidly learning to be most scared of.

"How could you permit this to happen? It's torture, pure and simple. No, actually, it's not. It's kidnapping, torture, and murder, and it is wholly unacceptable. You've killed your own Clerihorn, but it could just as easily have been Jake or me. You just stood back and let it happen. Why? How could you? I demand an answer, and it damn well needs to be a good one."

One of the three Elders got as far as, "Elder Nightingale, he..." before Holly cut him dead.

"He's an Elder. Same as you, and there are three of you. Why did you allow this to happen like this?"

"We only sought the truth."

"Well, you had it before, and now you've got it again. So what are you going to do with it?"

"No, we haven't," screamed Elder Nightingale, who was at this stage being restrained by two of the Elders in a tangle of twisted black robes. "Beldam manipulated this. It was a sham. We only got to hear her truth. I don't know how she did it, but she did. You should hold her responsible for the Clerihorn's death. Not me."

Holly remained exceedingly calm.

"She chose death. Sister Saurua — she had a name you know — chose death. She had been allowed to suffer too much for too long. She took my witchlight, while it was hers, and used it to end her suffering. I am honoured that she used my power to do so and shamed, because it need not have happened. You should be shamed too, but more so, because you're the cause of it."

There was something about Holly's strength of tone and demeanour. The echoing hall fell silent. Except, of course, for Elder Nightingale, who continued to remonstrate loudly. Brothers Lincoln and Wainthorpe, under the guidance of one of the three Elders, finally escorted him from the area.

With the loudly vocal Elder Nightingale gone, the remaining two Elders smoothed their robes and returned to Holly, who was checking that the still comatose Jake was okay, whilst sucking on her thumb. Being short, it gave her a certain childlike air, but this didn't last for long.

Before either of the two Elders had had a chance to speak, Holly, somewhat pointedly, said,

"Well?"

"Well?"

"Well, you can either explain yourselves, which I anticipate taking a rather long time if you are going to do it properly, and I do recommend that you do it properly. Or you can tell me where that leaves us — him, specifically." Holly nodded towards the unconscious Jake.

"Free to go," said the first Elder.

"With our apologies," added the second, when he caught sight of the tell-tale glint in Holly's eye.

"Is that all?" said Holly. The air around her was developing the glitter of frost, and the temperature in that part of the hall had plummeted below its normal comfortable levels. "I was expecting a bit more than '*Free to go*' and a mumbled apology. For example — and I wouldn't want to put words in your mouth — how about official confirmation that I am not responsible for Brother James' death? How about an official and lengthy apology to Jake Wortham because he was sucked into this medieval fiasco? Kidnapped, even. Oh, then there could be an official magic-bound promise that there will never, ever, be another Clerihorn, an official, retrospective apology to Sister Saurua for the damage done to her, both then and now, and the respectful handling of her remains, the ones over there that you all appear to be avoiding. Brother Nightingale — I have no intention of dignifying him with the title of Elder — needs to be muzzled, controlled, and watched. And I want..." Holly was about to say, "a full investigation into Brother James' activities at the time of his death," but was prevented from doing so by a feeble groan from Jake.

"I want to go home."

Holly hugged him and kissed him on the top of his head.

"So do I, sweetie," she said. Glaring at the two Elders, she concluded, "And I want an opportunity to complete my formal list of wants and have them officially recorded. But first, Jake and I are going home." And they did.

CHAPTER 20

In the kitchen at Basingfield Lane, two humans and two cats were gathered around the kitchen table. Or rather, the two humans, Holly and Jake, were seated at opposite ends of what suddenly seemed like a very long, bare wooden table and two cats, Barny and Grindlebones, were curled up snuggly side by side underneath it. Jake was gripping a large mug of steaming Horlicks, and Holly's left hand was cradling a triple single malt. She had expected it to be the other way around but discovered that she needed the scotch more than Jake, whilst he clearly craved the domestic comfort of the Horlicks. Perhaps it was because he had a more limited memory of events than Holly, or because he had a more limited understanding of them, or maybe both.

"So, tell me again what just happened?" Jake was asking the question of Holly, but his gaze was directed solely into his mug of Horlicks, thus avoiding eye contact with her. So far, he had successfully avoided making eye contact with Holly ever since they had returned from the High Hall of the Coven to Basingfield Lane. He hadn't even looked her in the eyes when he had dashed the first mug of Horlicks that she had magicked up onto the floor in a shower of broken pottery and oaty goodness and demanded that she make the Horlicks the traditional, old-fashioned, non-magic way.

The damage cleared up, the mug discreetly pieced back together, and the Horlicks made as requested, the pair of them found themselves at opposite ends of the table.

"You were picked up by the Coven and, in effect, held hostage, while they questioned me about the death of a Coven official. The one I've been telling you about, Brother James."

"And that freaky throne thing with spikes, people in spooky, medieval robes, and some sort of ugly, deformed creature, like a goblin? Did that happen too, or am I remembering the last horror film we watched together? And wasn't there a real sword, a big one?"

Holly took a gulp of scotch,

"You make it sound like something out of a sword and sorcery novel, but it wasn't. It was just the Coven going about its business. No goblins, just a badly damaged witch and the Coven's love of old-fashioned ceremony and dress-up. The important thing is I passed the test, and we're both home safe."

"You passed the test? I thought they were questioning you, not assessing your witch ability? What does 'passed the test' mean?"

"That I'm innocent of what they were trying to lay at my door."

"Innocent?" Jake did not seem especially convinced. Neither, ironically, was Holly. The Clerihorn had cleared her, but only she knew that she had helped things along in that direction to make sure the pure waters of innocence were not tainted in any way by what Barny and Grindlebones might, or might not, have done. She had reasoned that, if they had hunted down Brother James, it was only nature, red in tooth and claw, doing its thing. It was a wholly natural death. Except that, rather than a real rabbit meeting its natural fate, it was Brother James pretending to be a rabbit, which made things unduly complicated and icky. But it was a natural process, nevertheless. She was damned if she was going to let two helpless and innocent, or at least natural, cats be punished for being, umm, natural. Plus, she knew if they were implicated, the Coven would never believe that her familiars had acted without her knowledge or connivance. If they had been found guilty of his death, so would she have been.

"So, you're innocent?" Jake repeated the question with as little audible conviction as the previous time.

"The Clerihorn stated unequivocally that I had no hand in the death and no knowledge of it until after the event. It's official, and the Coven is bound to accept her words. That is the point of the torture, err torturous process."

Jake did not appear to hear her verbal stumble. "So what is this Clerihorn thing?"

"The ancient and disfigured witch you thought was a goblin."

"Oh. So what happened to her?"

"A long time back, she was badly damaged by some magic that went wrong. As of now, she's dead."

"Because of what happened?"

"Sort of, but the good point is, we're not."

"So, we could have been?"

Holly realised she had backed herself into a corner. If she said no, she'd be lying to Jake and would, in effect, be contradicting what she had just said. If she said yes, she was undermining her attempts at passing the event off as just more over-the-top Coven pomp and circumstance, and she would almost certainly freak Jake out.

Holly took another gulp of scotch,

"Not really, as such. We were largely nearly always safe. Mostly."

"So why…?"

"Tradition, ceremony, Coven pomposity, and the convoluted etiquette of witchcraft."

Jake said nothing more and returned to staring into his Horlicks. Holly pretended an intense interest in the amber depths of her single malt. She could not even begin to imagine how she could explain to Jake that they had both been at very real risk until she had thought to discreetly bend time a little during her walk to the blackthorn throne and had then managed to share some of her witchlight — up front and before the official start of the ritual — with the weakened Clerihorn. That way, the Clerihorn was better able to use Holly's main witchlight flow when it poured through her to protect Jake and Holly. It also gave Holly enough of a footprint within the Clerihorn's unstable mind to make sure she received the information she needed from Holly without having to blunder through her thoughts too deeply, either damaging Holly as badly as she had been damaged or inadvertently stumbling over the memory of two blood-stained and very full cats. This early intervention on Holly's part had also enabled her to ease the Clerihorn's pain a little. Ultimately though, combined with the amount of witchlight channelled through the Clerihorn and its raw undiluted strength, it had given the Clerihorn the power to decide on her future and free herself from a half-life she had been chained to for way too long. Holly felt relief for the old Clerihorn, but also a tinge of guilt, because it was, in effect, her Old Magic that had ended the witch's life. Then again, the ultimate responsibility lay with the Coven. Holly was just refuelling her righteous anger at both the clumsiness and callousness of the Coven's conduct when Jake spoke again.

"I'm sorry, Holly, I know it's unfair of me, but it's the magic's fault."

"Huh? I mean, what?" Holly was jolted from her scotch-deep reverie.

"It's true. I'm sorry, but if it wasn't for your magic, the whole, bloody black-magic court martial thing wouldn't have happened to us. We wouldn't have been put at risk. I wouldn't have ended up as some kind of sacrificial pawn in a game of arcane chess I don't understand the rules of. And before then, I wouldn't have been almost disembowelled by your grandmother's homicidal familiar or targeted by a magic-fuelled tornado. Life would have been simpler. There would have just been you and me. It's not that it's you. It's not even wholly me. It's the magic that is driving us further and further apart. It's stopping me from coping with normal relationship things. But then again, we don't have normal relationship things, just two more homicidal familiars and a house full of spells.

"I'm sorry, Holly. I'm really sorry, but I just can't cope with the magic. I thought I could learn to, but the more I try, the more difficult it becomes. Nothing has changed since yesterday, except for the worse. I still can't hack it, and wherever you are there's magic, and that's a big problem for me.

"Right now, I'm truly knackered, so I'm going to bed early because I have to, but I'm going to kip down in the spare room. When I wake up, whenever I wake up, I'm going back to my flat, and you're going to inform the Coven that we are no longer an item so that they are not tempted to come looking for me again. I don't know if that's true or not, but I need to feel safe, and I need a breather from all this magic stuff, so I can get my head sorted. It's all just too intense. I'm not used to it, and I'm not coping. It's not even fun any more." And with that, Jake put his empty mug down on the table and marched out of the kitchen without glancing back.

The two cats ignored his departure but unwrapped themselves to peer at Holly as drops of saltwater tumbled into her scotch. Their human was raining again. Fascinating.

CHAPTER 21

It was the beginning of June, Holly's birthday month, but she was in no mood for celebrating. The after-effects of The Clerihorn and Jake's dual departure had bitten deep. So deep, in fact, that the cataloguing at the library had been put on hold, along with what ought to be the pressing issues of the Polaroid, the prophecy book, the intercepted parcel, and the unfortunate Brother James. Holly knew she should be tackling all of them, let alone dealing with the library manifestations she had experienced, but she just couldn't motivate herself to do it.

The fact that she would be turning forty at some stage during the month — having been draped in magic and abandoned in a box as a baby meant that her precise birthday was a trifle vague — was not exactly helping her mood, either. Sarah was attempting to get her to celebrate the substantial anniversary in some way, but Holly was having none of it.

"I mean, Sarah, what's the point? What's really the point? Who wants to celebrate turning forty at the best of times? It's not exactly a kind birthday. But me? What I have I got to be happy about? The love of my life has left me — twice — and I'm once again on the shelf. Just this time, it's about to become a drab and dusty middle-aged shelf."

Sarah helpfully poured Holly another glass of red wine and tactfully said nothing.

"I really thought Jake and I were going to work. I mean, roses round the door and gazing lovingly at one another from our bath chairs when our hair has turned snow white sort of work. I believed that my wilderness years of failed and flailing relationships were behind me. I loved him. He loved me. We loved one another — *love* one another. It's supposed to work out."

"It still could, sweetie." Sarah did not sound especially convinced, but at least she was trying. "But even if things don't go as planned, there are plenty more hot, salty fish in the sea, wiggling their sexy fins and cute tails. And look at you. You may be on the point of toppling over into forty, but you could easily pass for thirty and, on a good day, even less. Or you could right up until the last couple of weeks. You've let yourself slide, Holly. You need to start making an effort again."

Holly regarded Sarah balefully over the top of her wine glass, but Sarah was on a roll.

"Why don't you treat the pair of us to a long weekend at a top-notch spa to celebrate your birthday? Mark won't mind, and I'd be delighted to accompany you. That way, you won't need to worry about some sort of party." Sarah was clearly enthused by her own idea, and her positivity was returning in spades. "It would be relaxing and fun, and you might regain a bit of your old sparkle. It would absolutely do you good, so you could consider it as therapeutic rather than celebratory, if you'd prefer. And who knows, if you book us into one of the super-duper luxury ones, you might come across an exceedingly wealthy silver fox. It's got to be worth a try."

"But I don't want some unknown old billionaire, however silver or platinum. I don't even want a young billionaire. I just want Jake." Holly almost burst into tears at this point, but she had been keeping it together for long enough now, so that all that happened was a slight wobble to her lower lip. She drank some more wine to conceal the tremble from Sarah.

Holly had really, really thought Jake was the one, and that without the wild magic malevolence of her grandmother poisoning her past relationships, as Ninanna had alleged, it was going to work. Then again, she could almost hear Ninanna saying, "Well yes, that's what I told you, my dear Holly, and if you chose to believe it, that's your choice. Maybe, however, I did nothing of the sort and the fact is, you are just incompetent when it comes to matters of the heart."

Holly pushed the thought from her head and tried to think positively about Jake. They'd had so much fun before Holly came out as a witch, and at first afterwards. Holly smiled to herself as she remembered Jake's childlike glee when she'd made him fly for the first time. He'd flown back and forth along the landing like a small boy trying out a new tricycle, albeit a tricycle with added wings. He'd had so much fun, he didn't want to come down.

"Happy thoughts at last?" Sarah enquired across the café table.

"Fond memories," Holly said and reached for her wine again.

A big part of the problem for Holly was the knowledge, or rather temptation, that she could have Jake back again at a click of her fingers, literally. Old Magic would bring him back to her, but then it wouldn't be real. It would just be the very magic that Jake now had such problems with taking him over and denying his free will. As much as she wanted Jake to come back to her, Holly didn't think she could live with that, even if it meant that Jake didn't come back.

Holly couldn't explain this to Sarah. In fact, Holly admitted to herself, she was still deceiving her best friend on a whole range of matters because she had never told her she was a witch. She had meant to, had been on the point of doing so, but given that coming out had worked so well with Jake — not — Holly was in no hurry to ruin any of her few successful relationships. Coming out to Sarah, or her father, come to that, was something for the future, if ever. Right now, she couldn't face it, couldn't face much of anything, if truth be told.

Holly had imagined that her outstanding ability with Old Magic was going to present her with limitless possibilities on a platter, and it did — it could — but she didn't want any of them. The only thing she wanted was Jake back, and magic couldn't give him back to her for real. Moreover, it was magic that had driven him away. Her magic. The power that ran through her and made her who she was – the woman that Jake didn't want any more. Another gulp of wine was called for, but the bottle was almost empty.

Sarah would have to go back to work soon. This was another of their lunchtime meet-ups in Cambridge, this time at a pavement café on King's Parade opposite King's College. So, there was little point in ordering another bottle. Having said that, Holly did briefly contemplate the possibility of sitting on her own in the sunshine with a fresh bottle all to herself but decided that would not be a sensible thing to do, even if she could adjust her own metabolism to stay sober. Solitary afternoon drinking did not seem a healthy way to pass the time.

Sarah was now at the stage of glancing rather regularly at her watch, so Holly assured her she would pay the bill, give serious consideration to the spa idea, and just have a cup of coffee before she went home. Then she shooed Sarah back off to work like a mother hen: a broody mother hen, a depressed, cage-trapped battery mother hen who was starting to pull out her own feathers. Oh shit. Her thoughts were running away with themselves again.

Holly gave herself a vigorous internal shaking — or as vigorous as she could manage at the moment — and ordered both her coffee and the bill. The coffee arrived quickly and Holly sat in the sun, admiring what little she could see of the ornate front of King's through the hordes of summer tourists and trying hard not to think too much. Then again, she needed to think, to drag herself out of her current depression. She fiddled listlessly with the pen that had come with the bill.

Sarah was not truly a lover of her job. It seemed to be mostly paperwork and computer screens. She had said jokingly on a number of occasions that if Holly wanted to donate a small fortune to her, she would happily chuck it all in. Her work did, however, appear to give her a sense of purpose and daily structure, both of which Holly was currently lacking.

Holly whirled the pen a little faster.

Jake certainly had a sense of purpose. As a successful vet, he was as tied to his work as he had once been to Holly. More so, currently, because he clearly wasn't tied to her anymore.

Holly's pen-fidgeting accelerated.

Thoughts of Jake at work made up Holly's mind for her. She was going to visit him, discreetly of course. She needed to see him to make sure he was well and to make sure the Coven was not coming anywhere near him. He wouldn't like it, but she needed to make sure he was protected. It was the only right thing to do. And, well, basically she just needed to see him.

The pen did a little flip of excitement in mid-air, and Holly suddenly realised she was being stared at by an open-mouthed four-year-old. Spinning a pencil by magic was the first thing Partridge had had her do. These days, it was almost an automatic process, and while she had been absorbed with her thoughts, the pen fiddling she had started manually had taken on a mid-air life of its own.

Holly slammed the pen down on the table and stuck her tongue out at the child, who retreated to her father with a garbled and unlikely tale about the magic lady at the table over there. By the time her father had looked up, Holly had paid her bill, shot into an adjacent alley, and was already on her way to spy on, or rather to see and look after, Jake.

CHAPTER 22

The broad Cambridgeshire sky was bright blue. White fluffy sheep-clouds ambled slowly through its wide, open space. Across the flat green fields below, real sheep were doing the same thing on more solid footing.

Holly was sitting on a hawthorn hedge basking in the early summer sunlight. Or, to be more specifically detailed, she was hovering, invisible, a centimetre above the prickly surface of the aforementioned hawthorn hedge and, for the first time in quite some time, she was enjoying herself immensely. The warmth of the sun and the simple satisfaction of basic, uncomplicated magic was working its own subtle non-magical spell on Holly's mood. The fact that she could also see Jake working amongst the real sheep down at field level was also a contributory factor to her positive spirits.

So far, Jake had attended to the veterinary needs of four sheep, and Holly had passed twenty contented minutes enjoying the view. For a man unaugmented by magic, he really was in excellent shape. Lean and muscular, without an inch of flab thanks to the regular work practices of an active, mostly outdoors vet. Holly could see his muscles flexing under the taut olive-green T-shirt he was wearing. The silver flecks in his thick black hair gave him an air of gravitas without ageing him too much. Holly was convinced he was going to mature into the fascinating silver fox type of man that Sarah was always on about. She just hoped she'd still be close enough to him to see it.

Holly was so focused on Jake that she hadn't noticed the bright yellow primroses dotting the field. There was nothing unusual about yellow primroses per se, but when Holly had first arrived at her hedgerow perch, the closely cropped grass in the field had shown no sign of yellow primrose activity. The first primrose had shot up rapidly when Jake removed his outer jacket, and a second had pushed its way up hopefully through the moist soil when he grabbed a sheep, thus emphasising the firm muscles that Holly so loved. Further primroses opened their expectant faces to the sun in an arc centred around Holly's hidden position and then began to pop up in ever-increasing numbers in a swathe that was headed slowly, but steadily towards Jake.

In her contentedly relaxed state, Holly failed to notice even one of the suddenly blossoming wildflowers. She did, however, register that Jake, at work as a vet and in his element, was calm, confident, and cheerful. Here was the man she had first met and fallen in love with, not the tense, grumpy, and frequently taciturn man she had recently found herself living with. Holly had to conclude that there were likely a number of reasons for this.

One, working out in the field with the sheep was therapeutic and did not involve magic. Two, at work and without the presence of magic, Jake felt relaxed and in control of things. Three, his work provided Jake with a sense of purpose and meaning that had been absent for him in an often random and magic-fuelled world. Four, Jake was good at what he did and liked doing it. Five, there was nothing and no one present (including Holly, as far as Jake was concerned) to remind him that the magic had not gone away as such but was still out there. He just couldn't see it. Number five made Holly pause.

Holly couldn't blame Jake for feeling uncomfortable around overt displays of magic. A world full of the stuff took a whole lot of getting used to. It had taken her a long time to adjust. If she was honest, she was still adjusting. The previous year everything had happened all at once: magic, suddenly found family, murderous grandmothers, and death – way too much death. It was only recently, once she had had time to be bored, that she had begun to accept things and adjust. The boredom had been useful in a way but had gone on for too long and was starting to edge towards lethargy and depression. From her previous career as a counsellor Holly knew the signs. Her depression was fortunately mild, but it was there, and she needed to acknowledge it and deal with it. She had become rudderless in an ocean of magical possibility, and she needed to get her sense of direction back.

Out in the increasingly yellow field, Jake, his back towards Holly's concealed position, was methodically tending to the needs of another bemused sheep. Holly watched as he finished with it and released it back to its flock, once more a happy and contented animal because it was back in a familiar environment that felt secure, even if there was a wolf waiting round the corner. Though of course, thought Holly, there wasn't, because there weren't wolves running wild and free in Cambridgeshire. Still, the metaphor worked, or would have worked if she weren't being quite so picky. She really did need to lighten up. She should take a leaf out of Jake's workbook and focus on concrete things that she wanted to do and were meaningful to her.

The question was, what did she want to do?

More than anything, Holly wanted to be back with Jake. The easy fun of this outdoor jaunt was beginning to give way to lengthening shadows of sadness. She could now see that she would have to let him go in order to give him the time and space to adjust to the magical new world she had plunged him into. Assuming he could adjust, of course. He clearly needed the apparent security of the mundane world while he came to terms with all that he had experienced under the auspices of witchlight. If she let him run back to his flock now, maybe, just maybe, he might be up to giving it another go with Holly in due course. Conversely, he might just decide that in addition to being a sheep, he also wanted to be an ostrich, stick his head in the sand, waggle his tail feathers in the air, and pretend that magic did not exist. So... it was painfully necessary to let him go for now. Again. Because hadn't she tried that before the Coven had kidnapped him and dragged him back into a maelstrom of witchlight and gothic columns? The bloody Coven was responsible for so much, both directly and indirectly.

Fine. There was little she could do about it. What she needed to do, for the time being at least, was legitimately use her Old Magic to protect Jake from other magic and the machinations of those with magic, like the Coven. An Old Magic cocoon of protection was doable and, to her way of thinking, acceptable. She wasn't using her power to coerce or secretly manipulate Jake. She was just looking after him, and she owed him that much.

Holly rose a few more centimetres above her hawthorn hedge. She stretched out her witchlight and a delicate veil of glittering white light extended over Jake. He couldn't see it and would never know it was there, but it would keep all magical interventions at bay for as long as the veil held. If the Coven wanted to contact Jake again, it would have to use strictly mundane means, and Jake could deal with those, or not, as he would any other day-to-day interactions. The witchlight veil also served to remove the temptation to influence Jake by magic that Holly had felt. She would have to withdraw the veil to use magic on Jake, and that would put him at increased risk from others, which she really wouldn't want. It also prevented her from using magic unconsciously on him, which she had worried she might inadvertently do. Holly had discovered early on that her power had a habit of seeping out round the edges of things if she was not exceptionally careful, and sometimes, even if she was.

Holly settled back down closer to the hedge. So, there was Jake, all safe and sound. She could see him, but she couldn't touch. Holly felt a little subdued at this point, but deep down in the core of her witchlight, she knew it was for the best.

So… with Jake looked after, Holly recognised she had to turn her attention on herself.

Yes, she was becoming depressed. Yes, she missed Jake badly, but she was no longer going to sit around moping about it. It was time to be active, find focus, and undertake meaningful activity, whatever that might be. She'd given up her mundane job the previous year when magic came calling. With hindsight, that may not have been such a good idea, but what was done, was done. Still, didn't she, in effect, have a temporary job at the Coven library? Okay, so she was not too keen on aiding the Coven any further than she needed to, but she hadn't taken on the work initially to help them. She had taken it on to help herself. The cataloguing still needed finishing and now there was the mystery of the appearance of Partridge, let alone the discovery of the Polaroid photo and the stolen photo album. Why had she allowed herself to abandon all of it? She was a powerful witch, but she had allowed her focus to slip badly. It wasn't good enough and quite clearly, she needed to motivate herself to give herself a good talking to. No one was going to do it for her. The only person she could rely on these days was herself.

"Consider yourself talked to," Holly said to herself, but not so loudly that Jake might hear. Somehow, it helped a little. She decided she needed to at least try to tackle her outstanding to-do list.

Preparing to leave, Holly blew Jake a silent kiss and was surprised to see a little yellow primrose blossom up where her imaginary kiss would have landed. She did a double take and suddenly noticed the spread of unseasonal early spring primroses actively blossoming in a semi-circle around Jake. Glancing back up the field, she could see a swathe of petal yellow flowing from her to Jake. Fortunately, Jake was still oblivious to the excessive floral display, but as he stepped forward towards yet another sheep, more pale-yellow flowers followed him like a trail of blossoming breadcrumbs.

Panicking slightly, Holly sharpened her vision and peered closely at one of the plants and then at another. There were more than enough to choose from. Each and every one twinkled ever so slightly with a delicate white frosting. Holly recognised the tell-tale. The primroses were the handiwork of her witchlight. She hadn't consciously intended it, obviously, but yet again it appeared her feral magic had an impetus all its own. The display was impressive and somewhat terrifying at the same time.

The sheep Jake was currently after eluded him, and he began to turn in order to catch it. Holly blinked rapidly and the primroses gently, but swiftly folded back into themselves and down into the grass. It seemed Jake hadn't noticed their unexpected arrival or sudden departure, but one bemused sheep found herself chewing on air just as she had expected a mouthful of succulent primula snack.

Holly breathed out. She hadn't realised she had been holding her breath. It really was time to go. With one last wistful glance towards Jake, Holly transported herself back to Basingfield Lane. She had work to do, and she needed to make preparations.

CHAPTER 23

Dressed smartly in a dark blue linen suit, cream silk blouse, and sensible, but stylish navy-blue kitten heels, Holly walked straight through the lift wall and into the library's spacious reception area. She was bracing herself for Cyril's contemptuous hiss and the increasingly — to Holly's mind at least — judgemental stare of his witch, but it was Marcus and Friedrich who were in place to witness Holly's return. This morning they appeared to be wearing matching diamante-studded orange leather dog collars.

"Back again, then?" warbled Marcus. "Nice of you to join us."

Holly smiled as sweetly as she could manage,

"I've been due a bit of me time. The Coven's hospitality can be a bit… overwhelming, but I'm back now and keen to get down into the old library to resume cataloguing. Is everything still ready for me down there?"

"Yup. All's ready and waiting. Though rather you than me, I have to say. We'll all be really glad when you get things sorted down there. Having said that, the long-awaited denouement will have to be postponed a little longer, I'm afraid. You've got another Coven invitation." Holly tensed. She couldn't help herself. Marcus must have noticed. "Don't worry, it's not as pointed as the last one. I heard on the grapevine how that went down. So macabre, love. We all sympathise — and quite understand the need for 'me time.' This invitation is relatively low-key and entails coffee and a biscuit (tea and other edibles are presumably available) with Elder Graham."

"Elder Graham?"

"Caprice Graham. She was appointed to the Inner Coven while you were off taking your 'me time.' Didn't you hear?"

"Err, no. Me time, remember? So where, exactly, is the invite for?"

"Here," Caprice's smooth tones flowed across the conversation. A scarlet edged portal had opened just above the middle of the reception foyer. "Want to come on over?" Caprice leaned out of the portal as if it was just a doorframe and held out her hand to Holly.

With a brief moment of hesitation, Holly grasped Caprice's hand and stepped forward and up into the illuminated opening. As she passed over the threshold, she found herself back in the black and white splendour of Graham's office. It was as imposing as ever, but perhaps, thought Holly, a little less ostentatious and a little classier. Holly couldn't quite put her finger on it, but the room décor looked more effortless and understated, but no less expensive. Perhaps it was the presence of a number of sympathetic, and clearly very pricey, antiques.

Caprice noticed Holly studying a glossy eighteenth century mahogany chest of drawers, now gracing a corner of her office.

"One of the perks of being a Coven Elder."

"Very nice, but you could have acquired something like this before. You didn't have to wait until you were elected an Elder, or is there a furniture code that accompanies the role?"

"True and no, no furniture code, but a piece like this is not, shall we say, my natural style. These days, though, I've got both standards and tradition to maintain. The Inner Coven is really into tradition."

"And you're really into the Inner Coven?"

"You could say that. I've spent years working for it. Making myself indispensable whilst dealing with, and cleaning up after, some of the Elders' more antique attitudes. But it's finally paid off. I'm a fully illuminated Elder. The first ever female Elder, I might add."

"The first ever woman? This is the twenty-first century, isn't it?"

"You'd think so, wouldn't you, but most of the Elders are really elderly, and they have commensurately antique viewpoints. It's taken a long time to break through and in the end, it was ultimately down to Elders Cavendish and Nightingale and their rather dubious approach in relation to you that got me here. The rest of the Elders thought the time was right to modernise and illuminate a woman. So here's little old me, Elder Graham, thanks to you. Last year's sudden revelation of an adult female witch with so much raw and feral power has really shaken things up round here. Plus, you've stirred things up a bit just by being you. Go girl."

"Oh well, I hadn't intended to, but I'll make no apologies for doing it."

"There's absolutely no need to apologise, Sister Holly. It was a long-standing need, let me assure you. History lies heavily on the Coven, and it needs to shake some of it off, it really does. You were the much-needed catalyst. I invited you here to acknowledge the recent poor behaviour of certain Coven members, to say thank you to you and to let you know that I am on your side. I'm rather hoping that you will be on mine."

Caprice sat down on the black leather sofa. Holly remained standing,

"Sides? Yours? I didn't know we were in a playground, or have more serious battle lines been drawn up somewhere?"

"Not battle lines, no," Caprice produced a brushed steel and glass cafetière of freshly prepared and highly aromatic coffee from mid-air and began pouring the coffee into a pair of elegant white and red bone china cups with matching saucers. They were antique in design, but brand new in appearance. Holly wanted to protest that she hadn't asked for coffee, but the smell was enticing, and coffee was exactly what she needed right now. She sat down on the sofa next to Caprice and accepted the cup and saucer, whilst inhaling gratefully. Caprice continued talking, "I just feel, Sister Holly, that, as women, we should stick together. I've worked damn hard to get where I am. I've spent more years than I care to admit at the Coven's beck and call, working very hard and extremely well, but it wasn't enough on its own.

"My witchlight is as strong as most Elders' and stronger than some I could mention, but it wasn't until your abnormal power set the cat amongst the pigeons — or should that be rabbits? — and highlighted the Inner Coven's galloping misogyny that anything happened. I reckon that sort of power and drain-unblocking ability will come in handy at some stage in the future.

"You should also be aware, if you're not already, that the Coven feels really uncomfortable in relation to you. At the moment, they recognise they have been in the wrong and are therefore backing off, but they don't trust you, your powers, or your ancestry. Many of them knew, had come across, or at least heard of Ninanna Beldam in the past and are wondering how much you are your own woman and how much you are your grandmother's granddaughter. You don't exactly take prisoners when it comes to your interactions with the Coven and its precious bureaucracy. There's also the unresolved mystery of Brer James.

"I realise you are more than capable of looking after yourself, but a friend on the inside can only be a good thing, right? What do you think?"

"This is really good coffee."

Caprice didn't conceal her disappointment,

"I was hoping for something a soupcon more positive. We could do one another a lot of good."

"I'll think about what you have said," Holly replied. "You do magic-up exceedingly good coffee, but right now I'm not sure I want to be dealing with uncertain sides and alliances. What I want to do is finish the cataloguing work I started and see what comes from it. Strategic alliances don't seem immediately relevant to building a book database, but I will think on what you have said. On *everything* you have said. That's a promise, but right now, this morning, I need to get back to the job in hand."

Reluctantly, Holly put down the remains of her cup of coffee, stood up, and walked towards the point of entry, or at least the place where she had last seen it. No scarlet-edged portal appeared, so Holly created her own exit, edged in white, slightly luminous mist.

"Thank you for the hospitality," she said and stepped back into the library reception area. From behind her, Holly heard Caprice call out,

"Think about what I've said, Sister Holly Beldam. I'm not going anywhere, and neither are you."

CHAPTER 24

Holly looked at Marcus, who peered back at her over the top of his reading glasses. The reading glasses were a fashion statement, rather than eye enhancement, as magic could have resolved any deficiencies in the eyeball department.

"Was that a promise or a threat?" he asked.

"I'm really not sure."

Marcus shrugged, "From what I know of the lady, it could be either. Ambition like hers requires a range of skills. You could always take some more 'me time.'"

"Nope." The word came out somewhat more emphatically than Holly was feeling, "I've got some cataloguing I need to finish."

"Whoa there. Are you sure you want to do this? I've never said anything before," Marcus leant across the reception desk conspiratorially and continued in a hissed whisper, "but it's become pretty intense down there at times recently. You sure you want to be dealing with that while you've got Crimson Caprice breathing down your neck?"

"Crimson what?"

"Caprice. Crimson Caprice. It's our name for the Coven's latest Elder. Appropriate, no?"

"Well, yes, I guess so, but what do you mean by 'intense?' Earlier, before my unexpected coffee break, you said 'rather you than me.' What are you getting at, exactly?"

Marcus retreated back across the reception desk, "Nothing, as such. Friedrich and I are a little hyper-sensitive at times. Goes with the territory." Marcus waggled a limp wristed hand to indicate extreme camp, but it seemed very contrived. Holly raised an eyebrow and stared directly at Marcus.

Marcus ratcheted up the faux campness in an attempt to convince Holly,

"Well, really, darling! We're both gay, you know, and highly sensitive little flowers under these trim and polished and, in his case," he glanced fondly at Friedrich, "rather furry, exteriors."

"If you say so. Feel free to be as sensitive as you want, but I'm still expecting you to explain your comments. Please."

Marcus shrugged again and reverted to his normal tones, "If you insist, but you aren't necessarily going to like it."

"And why not? Try me."

"Way to go, then. The deep library, where you are working, not the Coven document racks and archive on the upper levels — well, it's dark in more ways than one. Spend too long down there and — I don't know why I'm saying this bit because surely you of all people must know — you end up hearing and even seeing things. The library wasn't always just a library. It was completed as it is now when they built the mundane library up above. Parts of it, however, were there before. Underground pits have many uses, and not all of them are pleasant. Back in the day, before it was given up totally to book storage, it served as both a gaol and a court, as well as a museum and archive. Bad things happened there. Really bad things. They left their mark, and in the right circumstances, you can still feel their echoes."

"Okay, that's potentially dark, but why do you think I wouldn't like hearing about it? The Coven's interesting past is not exactly a state secret. Plus, I don't get scared easily, and I'm more than capable of looking after myself."

Marcus pulled a face, "Bear with me. I'm getting there. What I've described was the situation, as was, up until last year, when you and your grandmother trashed the place."

"But I restored everything. Put it all back together."

"Yes, you did, but something got changed in the process. The… echoes of the past, the manifestations became stronger and more frequent. It got so bad, you couldn't return a book by hand down there without bumping into someone you knew and who happened to be dead. I won't go down there anymore, with or without Friedrich." Marcus bent down and affectionately but nervously scratched his familiar's ears. "I'll work in the upper admin stacks, no problem, but I won't go through the portal into the deeper library. I don't know what you did, but something is going on down there. But I'm being stupid, because you know all this already, don't you? I mean, that's why the Coven brought you in? To sort out what's going on?"

Holly hesitated. The Coven's unexpected eagerness to employ her as a temporary cataloguing assistant suddenly took on a world of meaning she hadn't previously realised.

"I guess so. I mean, I hadn't really thought about it in quite that way."

Marcus shrugged again. Holly decided it was his default setting for most responses.

"I've always been surprised you don't take your familiar with you down into the library. Is it because of what you are doing down there, or is it just a wild magic thing? I'm sure Jemima's told you, but there's a good reason all the admin staff bring their familiars to work. They really do provide moral support and added focus. Plus, of course, some of them are really good at maintaining silence in the reading rooms."

Holly was going to repeat that she hadn't really thought about it in quite that way but wasn't particularly impressed by her own lack of verbal originality.

"I guess it's more of an Old or wild magic thing. Also, my familiar is more cat than witchlight accessory, and I wouldn't want him off running around the book stacks."

"Ah…" Marcus shrugged yet again, "but didn't you adopt Brother Mayflower's boy, Grindlebones? He's a witch-cat born and bred and should be fine down there."

At this point, Holly resorted to what was possibly a downright white lie, but hoped Grindlebones wouldn't be too offended, especially if it turned out to be true. "He's getting on a bit."

"Aren't we all, Sister. Tell me about it."

Holly seized her opportunity. "Yeah, and on that note, I probably ought to go before I get any older. Down into the library, that is. I really do need to make some progress on the, um, cataloguing."

This time, instead of a shrug, Marcus tapped the side of his nose in a knowing manner. "Fair do's. You know the way. Strong witchlight to you."

Holly smiled at Marcus, left the reception area, and walked briskly towards the pentagram portal. After all of Marcus's comments, and as enlightening as some of them had been, Holly's stomach was starting to tense. What might be waiting for her down there? Something? Someone? Or was it just the dry conversation of the books that she was becoming used to, and that was so alarming everyone else?

Holly stepped into the portal and began the descent. It was uneventful, as was her arrival. The lights came on. Nothing and nobody was waiting for her. There were just a lot of books.

Where were the normally vocal books? Holly listened for the dry rustling in her head. Nothing.

"Are you there, um, here?"

There was further silence. Not the slightest rustle. Then, the voice in Holly's head came through loud and clear, "We are always here."

Holly had wanted to hear them, but now was not sure this was exactly comforting.

"Where, precisely, is here? In my head or in the library?"

"Both, as we have confirmed before, but we are stronger in the library when you are in the library."

"Right. So, if you are always in my head, did you hear the conversation I had upstairs?"

"No."

"Really?"

"We are with you. We are not you. Your subconscious has become more adept at blocking us. We cannot use your senses unless you permit us to."

Holly was unexpectedly relieved and subconsciously patted her subconscious on the back. "Sure?"

"Of course."

"I had wondered…"

"…and now you are wondering something else?"

Holly repeated the salient points of her conversation with Marcus.

The books considered the information and then said, "So, maybe we have been heard more often than we thought. Our build-up has been slow and steady, but the introduction of your Old Magic freed and augmented us. We are stronger since because of it."

"So, you are telling me that is all there is to this? That you're the reason all the reception staff cling to their familiars like sentient comfort blankets?"

"We cannot answer for their choices. You hear us because of our inherent connection. We do not knowingly communicate directly with the others." The dry tone of the voice began to take on a more human depth, and Holly found herself once more talking to the Partridge aspect of the consciousness. It made her happy and sad at the same time. "Don't forget, Holly girl, I did tell you that you needed to work out how you saw me when I wasn't there. It wasn't us that made you see me. So, how's the investigation working out for you?"

Holly looked down at her feet. It was like being tutored by Partridge all over again.

"Um, it's not. I've been busy. Distracted by things. I've had stuff. Personal. If you're in my head, you must know."

The voice became dry and rustling once more. "We have said. We can no longer access your senses unless you choose it. Pages do not see or hear."

"Isn't that horribly claustrophobic?"

"We do not understand the question. Claustrophobia is an emotion in response to a physical situation. We have neither. We are knowledge, facts, echoes of what was."

"But you've got to be more than that. You've got my memories inside you. You said. My memories are frequently emotional. And, anyway, you are a conscious entity. You react."

"Yes and no. It's complicated." The last three words were in Partridge's voice. Holly had a feeling that the books were using him to distract her. It was almost certainly working.

Holly attempted to refocus. "Look, I need answers. I've told you the conversation I had upstairs. I need to know what's unnerving the staff. If you are not causing the visible manifestations, what is?"

"We can only explain what we know."

"Yes, but it's happening in the library. You are part of it."

"We have acknowledged that your Old Magic enhanced us. The recent experiences of your receptionists are therefore not unexpected, but you yourself have seen a visual manifestation that we did not create. It is not unreasonable to assume that the other manifestations spoken about were caused by the same thing, and that this thing may also have been enhanced by the release of so much wild magic in so short a space of time."

"But you don't know this?"

"We only know what we know."

" I know. You've said, already. Visual hallucinations in the library seemed up your street, somehow."

The voice did not respond. Holly did, however, hear a faint rustling. It made her think of Marcus shrugging his shoulders.

Holly carried on. "What about some things I found in the library? A book of prophecy and a photo of me, taken when I was little. I found them here, but they are connected to me and to a Coven official who was murdered near to where I live. It's a book. It's in the library. You must know something about that?"

"Many of these things are unconnected to us, but the book was briefly known to us. Then it was taken away and shielded from us."

Holly's heart raced.

"So, you're telling me that something or someone deliberately concealed it?"

The voice was now a mixture of Partridge and the dry, bookish voice,

"You keep asking us to know what we do not know. Perhaps you should ask us what we do know?"

"So, what do you know?"

"We are thoughts and memories and words once spoken. We know the past."

"I need to know what's happening now, not past events."

"Sometimes one can affect the other." The words were now wholly in Partridge's somewhat exasperated tones. "History lies heavy on the Coven."

"That's what Caprice said."

"Caprice? Crimson Caprice? She would know."

"What does that mean? That I should ask Caprice or what? Can't you give me a straight, honest answer?"

"All our answers are honest, girlie, and they are as straight as a non-corporeal, hive-minded, trace entity can manage. Trust me."

"I want to, and that's part of the problem." Holly's voice cracked a little, "I mean, you're not who you sound like, are you? You're not really Partridge."

"I am a partial imprint, all that is left behind of… me. I'm as good as it gets, and I can tell you things I, we, know. I can tell you about the history of the library. It wasn't always a library. Underground pits have many uses."

"Wait a moment. First you echo Caprice Graham, then you repeat what Marcus said. Is that all this conversation is — echoes of what others have already said?"

"Maybe, but it doesn't make these things any less true. History was real when it was happening. As an example, witch trials have been held down here. Remember, I told you when I was alive that there had been bad, dark times in our past. Too many bad times took place here: trials, interrogations, inquisitions. The last Clerihorn was conducted here. It went so badly wrong the Coven swore it would never hold another. Such things leave resonances of their own behind them. But this was in the days before the library was as it now is. There were fewer books here then. Any such resonances from that time are weak within us. From what you say, it seems the library staff don't know the fuller picture, but the Librarian should. He is an Elder. Has he never said anything?"

"Actually, I've never met him."

"Really?"

"Really."

"If there are unexplained things taking place in his library, and you're supposed to be sorting them out for him, maybe you should."

"Maybe I should, but I also need to do some further book research myself. That's what I originally came down here to do."

"No one's stopping you on either count, girlie. You summoned us, remember? You can talk to us again, if you need to. We're not going anywhere."

It was Holly's turn to shrug. "So, I'd best be getting on with it then."

There was no further response, and Holly realised she was listening to the empty silence of absence.

CHAPTER 25

Holly slowly and thoughtfully made her way through the book stacks of the old library to where a desk, chair, and her computer equipment had remained set up since her last visit. She had been away from the library for too long. Her conversation with Partridge, or rather the books' consciousness or non-consciousness, or whatever damn thing it thought it was, had highlighted that. It was time to look for some answers, and the collected history books of the library seemed as good a place as any to begin in earnest. Then again, most of the books in the library were old and therefore inherently historical. Maybe a full witchlight trawl through the remaining books she hadn't yet catalogued would be more effective than mundane review and computer processes alone, or even the half-and-half approach she had used previously.

Looked at from another angle, however, and given what little Holly knew of the impact of her use of Old Magic to absorb books in the past, maybe the ramifications of a full-blown witchlight search were really not desirable. Why was life never simple?

In the end, Holly created a shield of frosted white witchlight around both her and the area of the library in which she was working and then planned to absorb and catalogue all the relevant books in that area using Old Magic. It was easily done, she only had to will it so, but it was not as quick as absorbing the entire library at one go. It was, however, hopefully safer as the effects of Old Magic were at least contained and limited.

Under the protection of the sparkling eldritch dome, Holly relaxed and envisioned her Witchlight flowing out of her and then mentally directed it to identify, catalogue, and absorb all the books and manuscripts in the protected area that were historical, related to the history of witchcraft, or were just plain old. She imagined releasing the witchlight in waves of bright, white light that rhythmically rolled away and lapped at the books and documents on the shelves. As she imagined it, it happened. And then, the flow of her witchlight inverted, and the waves of light rolled back to her, bringing information with them. The protective shield meant that the information was the only thing the waves brought back, plus it was manageable, and her own power couldn't accidentally splash or soak into other parts of the deep library.

Holly repeated the process a number of times in different areas of the library until she was satisfied that all the books that might be considered remotely historical had been captured. She then repeated the entire safely cloaked process for anything that related to prophecy directly or indirectly, in case she had missed anything the first time around. There were still, perhaps not surprisingly, an exceedingly small number of books involved. But then, fortune telling wasn't a skill set normally associated with witch power and, by rights, she had already absorbed all of the books she was looking for.

When that was done, Holly sat back and considered what remained to be catalogued book-wise, as well as what she now knew from the books so far absorbed. The first part was easily done, but slightly dispiriting. Across all her cataloguing visits, and the various methods she had employed to process books, she had succeeded in cataloguing a little under half the books in the entire collection. There were still many, many books waiting to be dealt with. So many, in fact, that Holly did not want to put an accurate figure on it in case the sheer volume of what remained to be tackled demotivated her even further. Instead, she concentrated on the fact that she was almost half-way through, because that had to count for something.

The second part of the exercise was also somewhat spirit-dampening. She had absorbed a sizeable amount of information, but, she concluded, there was no way of reviewing it at one go or even browsing through it. As before, if she needed to know something in particular or thought directly about a specific issue, the information was suddenly there. But a general overview seemed to be beyond her, however hard she tried.

Resigned to her fate. Holly sat and thought about prophecies and the legitimacy of them. The books largely seemed to be saying that prophecy was not genuine and not something a witch could realistically perform. There were one or two manuscripts that referenced the prophecies she had come across earlier, and the name of Samuel Lighthowlers cropped up on a couple of occasions. But overall, there was nothing new or as detailed as the book she already had. Then she realised with a jolt that the book of diary excerpts and other prophecies she had found previously, the one with the polaroid photo in it, was not amongst the collection she had just absorbed. She had kept the photo with her when she left the library, but she had returned the book to its shelf. She was sure of it, but as hard as she thought about the book, she couldn't find it.

Concerned, she checked the section of the computerised database she had been creating when she had first found the book. On the screen appeared the words, "Untitled, faded tan leather binding, anonymously collected prophecies — gathering of Old Magic?" and a shelf location. Holly immediately transported herself to the shelf in question, but the book wasn't there. She checked the adjoining shelves visually and then by magic and finally ran a full tracer spell, but there was no evidence the book had ever existed.

Perhaps she had taken the book home and just forgotten she had done so. The tracer spell would normally have picked that up, but the Old Magic protection surrounding both her homes was highly effective and could easily be blocking her search. There was no point in worrying about it now, she would just have to repeat her search later once she was back home, at either and both homes.

Perhaps she should spend some time considering the history side of things, seeing as both Partridge and Caprice had placed emphasis on it. She focused her thoughts on that.

The information that filled her head when she considered the history of the Coven was unexpectedly dark. Holly could only conclude that she would need several stiff drinks when she finished for the day. She even considered pouring herself one with immediate effect but knew the books didn't like fluids being consumed or even present amongst them.

When the then very-much-alive Partridge had first explained something about witchcraft's past to Holly, he had said there were dark things that organised witchery was not proud of. Considering these things en masse, even from a slightly detached historical perspective, made Holly feel ill.

Some of the contemporary records were the worst, and it was here that Holly found details of the last Clerihorn — or at least the last Clerihorn prior to her own debacle. It made for grim reading.

It had taken place in 1917. The use of one in the twentieth century surprised Holly. The ritual felt as if it belonged firmly in the Middle Ages. The Great War had affected the world of witchery as much as the broader mundane world, and perhaps the brutality and bloodshed of the conflict had fuelled The British Coven's ensuing actions. It had certainly triggered it.

The Coven was convinced they had a spy in their midst, but they had no real evidence to prove who it was. Fingers were pointed at a number of individuals, but the accusation of guilt finally settled around the shoulders of a Sister Victoria Saurua, a witch of Anglo-Indian descent and a known suffragette, both grounds for distrust as far as the Inner Coven of the time was concerned. Saurua's mixed race seemed an especial issue for the Coven. Her father was English, but her mother was Indian, which meant the line of Saurua's witchlight was also Indian. To the Coven's biasedly British and also no-doubt racist way of thinking, this made it, and her, both alien and unknown and consequently inherently untrustworthy. She also had the misfortune to be a woman and therefore made the ideal scapegoat, though she emphatically and repeatedly denied any involvement with the German Empire.

Despite identifying Victoria Saurua as the guilty party, the Coven still had a problem. There was no real evidence to support the charges of spying for the Imperial Germanic Coven they had brought against her. It was now that the impersonal wheels of the British war machine took effect. Or perhaps it was the equally callous, but all too personal machinations of the British Coven. In either event, it was proposed that a Clerihorn be convened to extract the truth from her. The ritual hadn't been held for at least fifty years, and a certain Elder Nightingale volunteered to set it up. Holly couldn't tell from the documents if this was the same Elder Nightingale who had so enthusiastically involved himself in her Clerihorn or whether he was a relative, but it didn't totally surprise her to find the name of Nightingale linking the two events. It was something she would look into at a later date, if she felt she needed to.

Regardless of who this Elder Nightingale was, he clearly had a taste for the truly gothic. For reasons presumably clear to him, he chose to run The Clerihorn in accordance with recorded Medieval practices, abandoning any refinement that had been adopted in the intervening centuries. Holly's horrendous throne of Blackthorn had been preceded by an original Iron Maiden, with spikes cleaned and sharpened for the occasion. The witch chosen to fulfil the role of Clerihorn and to channel Saurua's witchlight was Elder Nightingale's young son, who had barely come into his own full witchlight. In many ways, he was the required empty vessel, but also a very weak one.

Whether it was the weakness of the chosen Clerihorn, or whether other issues were involved, it wasn't clear to Holly, but, regardless, the ritual went hideously wrong. Too much witchlight was drained from Sister Saurua, leaving her powerless to protect herself from the physical agony of the Iron Maiden. The young Clerihorn was unable to contain the excess power pulled from Saurua, and it burned him up from the inside out, an excruciatingly painful death that at least ended in oblivion for the sufferer, but left Saurua's witchlight uncontained. Crushed and pierced within the Maiden, Saurua was physically maimed and brain damaged and unable to protect herself. What the Maiden didn't destroy, the backlash from her uncontrolled witchlight implosion did. Somehow, she remained alive but was little more than a misshapen human vegetable, with only a vestigial trace of witchlight. It was probably this last whisper of witchlight that had enabled her to survive in the first place. Magic was a double-edged sword in this context. She almost certainly would have been better off dead, but the Coven, for reasons of its own, chose to use its collective witchlight to keep her alive for a further ninety-three years until it produced her as the empty vessel to be filled with Holly's wild magic at the most recent Clerihorn ritual.

Eighteen months after Saurua's catastrophic Clerihorn, the identity of the real spy was uncovered by more conventional mundane means. Her suffering had been, and continued to be, wholly without justification. The contemporary account Holly was reading needed a positive outcome, however, and the swift action of Elder Nightingale, despite the appalling fate of his son, was described as saving Sister Saurua from almost certain death. He became the hero of the hour. Her continued existence, in whatever state, served to highlight his allegedly amazing valour in the face of great personal tragedy. Perhaps it was not so surprising, therefore, that her shattered and mutilated body was maintained by the Coven.

Holly felt physically sick at the whole bloody situation and its aftermath. She really needed fresh air and soon. Getting up in a hurry, she suddenly realised she was no longer alone. Standing ten feet or more away from her, with her back against a stack of full bookshelves, was a young woman, apparently in her twenties, wearing a non-descript long grey dress. Slim, tanned, dark eyed and with long, thick, straight black hair she was both familiar and unknown.

"Hello," called out Holly. "Can I help you?"

The woman stared fixedly at Holly but said nothing.

"Is there anything I can do for you?" Holly tried again. The woman remained silent, but slowly closed her eyes. When she opened them again they glowed with white light. The light spread and stained her hair equally white. It was then that Holly recognised her,

"Sister Saurua?"

The woman smiled and stepped sideways, back into the shadows between the shelf stacks, disappearing in the process.

Holly hurried forward to where she had been, but there was no longer anyone there. Perplexed, Holly stood on the exact spot the woman had been occupying and ran a search spell. As she had almost expected, the only human entity in the lower library was herself. She continued to stand unmoving, partially listening for retreating footsteps and partially wondering what to do next. At first there was nothing. Then she felt, rather than heard, a faint vibration that rapidly became a tingling in the soles of her feet. In the second or so it took her to consider what she was feeling and what it might mean, the tingling had escalated to an uncomfortable burning sensation, as if something hot was being drawn down through her feet. It was then that Holly realised her own witchlight was being drained from her. With an uncontrolled yelp she leapt away from the spot she was standing on. The sensation in her feet immediately ceased.

Holly braced herself for a further assault, but nothing else took place. Her feet didn't tingle or burn. The voices in her head remained mute, and the library itself was as silent as an abandoned grave. She checked. There was no trace of Old Magic, or even standard magic, having been used.

"Was that you?" she said out loud, but really to the dry voices in her head. More silence. Holly focused on her internal lodgers, "I said, was that you?"

"We have done nothing. What has occurred?"

"I saw someone who apparently wasn't there."

"It happens down here."

"So I gather. Were you, are you, responsible?"

"No."

"Someone or something also tried to siphon off some of my witchlight. Was that you?"

"Again, no."

No joy there, then. Holly figured she ought to stop her cataloguing activities for the day in order to pursue this matter further and without too much time getting between the event and the investigation. If nothing else, it really was time she sought a meeting with The Librarian.

Despite a growing sense of urgency, she tidied up her work area before leaving. She didn't like leaving things in a mess and clearing up using magic was pretty much instant. She didn't even bother to wave her hand in the general direction of her desk.

The journey up from the lower library through the portal was as long as it was, but it felt infuriatingly slow. On arrival in the upper records section of the library, Holly almost transported herself directly into the reception area, but managed to control herself sufficiently to observe protocol and walk briskly to the front desk where Marcus and Friedrich had now been replaced by Jemima and Cyril. Cyril hissed.

"Hi," Holly smiled thinly and took a gamble that everything Marcus had confided to her was kosher and common knowledge amongst the staff. "There's just been another manifestation in the old library. I need to meet with The Librarian."

"Oh," Jemima blanched, but whether it was mention of another sighting or of The Librarian, Holly wasn't too sure. "I'm really not certain that that is at all possible. The Librarian doesn't meet with anyone below the rank of Elder, and not always then. I'm sure I've said."

"Yes, you did mention it, but things are escalating down there, and I really do need to see him. Things aren't, erm, going according to plan. If I can't talk to him, I'll have to go direct to the Inner Coven."

Cyril wrapped himself round and round his witch. Jemima tugged absently at the bit of Cyril that was coiled around her neck the way one might try to loosen a scarf that had become too tight.

"Well, I can ask, of course, but to be honest, I don't think you'll have any joy unless you do get a Coven Elder to intervene for you."

Holly swore under her breath. She really didn't want to go cap in hand to Caprice Graham quite so soon.

"Could you just ask, please?"

"Well, yes, I can, but…"

Holly didn't hear the rest of the sentence. She had started to tingle again, but this wasn't the unpleasant feeling of witchlight flowing away through her feet. This was the all-over warning vibration that indicated one of her magic wards had been tampered with.

Holly permitted the vibrations to grow deeper and stronger while she willed herself not to panic. An image came through to her. It wasn't the protective veil that surrounded Jake that had been triggered, it was the warding that surrounded the cottage in Oxfordshire. Without waiting further and whilst hurling a brief, "Sorry, I've got to dash" at Jemima and Cyril, Holly transported herself straight to the Cottage.

CHAPTER 26

Holly arrived, with just the slightest twinkle of frosted white light, behind a large mauve, florally abundant rhododendron in the back garden of the cottage. Immediately, she checked the protection wards around the cottage. Nothing seemed to have been breached. To be on the safe side, she scrutinised the inside of the building while remaining outside in the garden. Once again, nothing seemed to be out of place.

Feeling slightly more confidant, though none the less perturbed, Holly transported herself directly in to the spotless, flag-stoned kitchen and then checked the cottage in person from the inside out including — especially — the inner room decorated with a large pentagram and extra warding spells where her grandmother's remains were held. All was well, but the alarm had indicated that someone or something had made contact with the protective magic around the cottage. As per her experience in the library, there were none of the tell-tale signs that indicated that either standard witchlight or Old Magic had been used, but there was also no evidence of a real-life physical presence.

Holly was debating with herself what to do next when the all-over warning tingle began again. This time the warning was coming from the house in Cambridgeshire. Holly re-sealed the cottage and switched counties in another brief flash of frost-edged white. She arrived in the field behind the Basingfield house just in time to see a lithe black and white cat streaking away from the house and across the field in front of her. At least Barny was safe, if rather startled. Holly wondered where Grindlebones was.

Retracing Barny's rapid exit, Holly walked briskly across the field, levitated less than discreetly over the back-garden fence (the neighbours were all out at work, so there was little chance of being seen), and then trotted through her florally fragrant back garden.

The warding magic was intact, the back of the house seemed untampered with, and the back door into the kitchen was firmly locked. As before, Holly checked the inside of the house from the outside, before transporting herself into her modern, gleaming kitchen. A thorough and personal check of all the rooms in the house reassured her that all was well, though she couldn't find any sign of Grindlebones. She guessed he must have been out of the house when the alarm went off.

Holly moved back through the house to the front door, which she opened with the aim of undertaking a physical inspection of the front of the house from the outside. She was startled to find Grindlebones sitting on the external front door mat, directly outside the front door, and next to a brown, rectangular object. Her surprise took a deep intake of breath when she realised that the object in question was the missing scrapbook of prophecies, unwrapped and unprotected and, well, just lying there next to the ginger cat.

Perplexed, Holly bent down to retrieve the book, and in the process, automatically scratched the top of Grindlebones' head. The cat did not respond but continued to stare into space or at the lower leaves of a nearby rose bush. It was difficult to work out which.

Holly walked over to the rose bush to inspect it but could see nothing there. As she crossed back in front of Grindlebones, she finally picked up a fading sense of something akin to Old Magic, like the last vestiges of a frail frost on an early spring morning. When she looked closely, there was the merest glimmer of crystalline white. It felt oddly like an echo of her own witchlight, mixed with something that was not witchlight at all.

Holly glanced back down at Grindlebones. His gaze was unbroken, and his large yellow eyes were staring straight through her as if she wasn't there. Then he began to make a plaintive mewing sound she hadn't heard since she had first brought him home following Partridge's death.

"What is it, boy?" but Grindlebones ignored her and carried on staring into nowhere or perhaps, Holly suddenly realised, at the last evaporating traces of the not-quite her witchlight.

It was at this moment that several thoughts struck Holly all at once (she really wished things would start cropping up one thing at a time). She had last seen the prophecy book in the library, from where it had apparently disappeared. Someone or something in the library had tried to draw off some of her witchlight. The only sign of a magical presence close to the house, other than her own, was this trace of power that was like hers, but wasn't quite, and which led away from the book that had come from the library. Was it her stolen witchlight that was mixed with something else, and would following it, therefore, lead back to the library?

Grindlebones' mewing was getting louder and, although he hadn't moved or changed his focus, he now seemed to be straining forward as if he really wanted to go in that direction but was unable to. She sensed his need to follow the fading trail.

"What is it, Grindlebones? Do you want to follow the magic? Shall the pair of us do that?"

Holly strongly doubted that what she was about to do was even remotely sensible, but the urge to follow the trail before it disappeared was strong. She sensed that was the issue with Grindlebones, and she was convinced she was not going to get any answers about an increasingly complex situation via any other methods.

Concentrating on the last few and rapidly fading echoes of magic, Holly stepped forward and visualised herself and Grindlebones following it. The instant she moved, the prophecy book gripped firmly in one hand, she heard Grindlebones meow and from the corner of her eye, saw him stand up, stretch, and fall into place beside her.

Holly maintained her focus on the magic and continued to move forward, the world around her blurring at the edges of her vision. She could feel the surrounding landscape changing, but, like Grindlebones earlier, did not shift her gaze from the thin trail of magic.

The environment suddenly grew darker, and the trail stopped. Holly stopped moving, and with a soft, furry thump, Grindlebones collided with the backs of Holly's legs and stopped moving forward too. They were indoors somewhere and standing in a narrow and gloomy corridor. To her left, the corridor stretched away towards a distant but familiar light that glowed like a clear summer's morning. Holly recognised her own handiwork. It was the light she had installed in the library the previous year. She could only assume, therefore, that she and Grindlebones were underground and that, in that direction, the tunnel fed into the lower library.

To Holly and Grindlebones' right, the corridor climbed gently upwards, growing less and less gloomy as it rose. Further along, the decoration and detail seemed Victorian and at the end of the corridor, where it apparently made a sharp right-hand bend, there was a subdued yellow glow that resembled candlelight but wasn't. It reminded Holly of the lighting in the Coven's grand hall. Along the sides of the corridor in that direction were what looked like old-fashioned gas lamps, but the dim light that burned in each of them was clearly fuelled by witchlight.

In front of Holly and Grindlebones, and slightly to their right, was an old and very dirty door. It had once boasted a glossy mahogany surface and intricately inlaid panels, but the wood was now dry and cracked. There was a dull brass plaque in the middle of the door at head height — or at least head height for the average person. Holly had to crane her neck to try to read it, but it did no good. The brass was so tarnished, she couldn't make out the etched letters on the plate.

In the meantime, Grindlebones had sidled around Holly's legs and was now sitting directly in front of the door, appearing to stare through it in much the same way that he had sat on her front door mat staring into space. Holly came up beside him. With a brief flare of white light, she cleaned the letters etched into the plaque so that they shone out, bright and brassy, from the corroded surround. They now clearly spelled out "Office of Head of Library."

Well, that confirmed it, Holly thought. The trail of almost-but-not-quite witchlight had led back to the library — or at least to a corridor which joined the library to someplace else. Holly had a feeling the someplace else was the mock gothic hall of the Coven. A Head Librarian who wouldn't get out of bed for anyone less than an Elder was bound to want his office near the perceived seat of power. It was interesting that she hadn't come across this corridor previously. She sensed an old but strong masking spell further down the corridor closer to the library.

Holly glanced down at Grindlebones, who had once again started to mew pitifully and was now scraping at the door with his front left paw. His claws were beginning to leave gouge marks in the woodwork.

"Okay, Grindlebones. It looks like you and I are never going to be grand enough to be given an official appointment with the Head Librarian. What do you say? Shall we simply announce ourselves?"

Grindlebones meowed loudly, and Holly tossed a focused ball of white light at the door, which obligingly opened with a pop, a loud groan, the squealing of stiffened hinges, and an outward exhalation of dusty and not-exactly-fresh-smelling air. Grindlebones shot forward through the open door, and Holly followed on after supplying ambient illumination. There was no natural, or even artificial, light within the office.

At first glance the large room appeared unoccupied and abandoned. There was dust over every available surface, and the smell of mildew and rot was very strong. Holly noticed a line of pseudo gas lamps along two of the walls and used her witchlight to illuminate them in much the same way as the lamps in the corridor had been lit.

Holly could now see Grindlebones crouched expectantly in a corner of the room and a large and exceptionally filthy desk in the middle of it. The dust was thick over most of the desktop except for a rectangular book-shaped and dust-free space in the middle of it that exactly matched the size and shape of the prophecy book in her hand. Behind the desk was a large, high-backed leather chair. The back was turned to face Holly so that anyone sitting in it would be shielded from someone entering the office via the door.

Holly had seen no end of horror films and knew that turning round old concealing chairs in abandoned places led to bad outcomes, but she had to know. Fingers of white witchlight flowed away from Holly's hands towards the chair, seized hold of the back and legs, and slowly but surely turned the chair around to face her. Slouched in the seat, empty eye sockets pointing directly towards her was, guessed Holly, The Head of The Library. He was clearly very dead and, judging from the skeletal remains that were visible through a long, once-black gown, as well as the skull that was confronting her, had been very dead for quite some time. Years even. No wonder he never accepted appointments.

Holly was fascinated and repulsed by the skeletal remains in equal measure and so engrossed that she didn't notice the figure emerging from the shadows in the far corner of the office nearest the library. It moved forward silently, drawing closer to Holly and watched only by Grindlebones on the opposite side of the room. It had almost reached Holly when Grindlebones yowled. Holly looked up, then down and up again, and found herself within a foot of the slim, dark-haired woman she had earlier seen in the library. This close, Holly could see that the grey dress she was wearing had once been white. It was now filthy and boasted a variety of unpleasant looking stains that could easily be old, dried blood and other leaked bodily fluids.

This close and personal, Holly could see the face quite clearly, and this time there was no doubt. She had last seen it crowned with long white hair and illuminated from within by her own witchlight. It was Sister Victoria Saurua, whom Holly knew to be as seriously dead as the desiccated remains seated at the desk.

CHAPTER 27

Holly spoke first,
"I don't believe in ghosts, so you're going to have to explain what I am seeing."

"I am not a ghost. I am a… vestigial essence… I believe. Sister Ninanna Beldam built up her power by trapping vestigial traces of life and witchlight in the physical remains of otherwise dead individuals. Whilst I am physically dead, this aspect of me has also been trapped, not in my remains, but in the accumulated magic of the library."

Holly thought hard about the library voices in her head and before she could open her mouth a second time, the dry tones said to her, slowly and unambiguously,

"No. She is not a part of us."

Holly stared into the dark eyes of the figure standing in front of her,

"The Library begs to differ. It says you are not a part of it. Would you care to revisit your explanation?"

The woman glided closer to her. Holly contemplated backing up but thought it would look like fear. She chose to stand her ground.

The woman continued, "I will explain in what greater detail is available to me, but that which I tell you is true. I am what is left of myself, Sister Victoria Gita Saurua. I am part of what surrounds us, the physical space that is now the library, but was once otherwise. I am trapped in this location, this fabric of place, but I am not a part of any essence the Library may have developed. I preceded it."

There was much rustling at the back of Holly's head, but no words formed. Holly decided to use the silence to clarify a few points of her own,

"Fine, if you say so. It sounds rather macabrely poetic, but I'd really like to know a little more precisely what you are and who that is," she pointed to the crumbling skeleton in the chair, "and how you know so much about Ninanna Beldam. I have time, so there is no need to skimp on the words, but I would like you to keep things strictly truthful, please."

Whilst she waited for a response, Holly used her magic to whisk away a pile of mouldering books from a spare chair, cleaned the chair up, had second thoughts, and then produced a clean, modern and comfortable leather armchair that she then sat herself in. A slim, pale wooden side table with a warm teapot full of Earl Grey tea and a delicate porcelain cup and saucer perched on it appeared alongside Holly and the chair.

"Do you want one?" Holly pointed in the direction of the tea things.

"No. I am non-corporeal. This body is a construct of light. But thank you for asking. I am still able to appreciate the niceties of life, unlike my friend here." Saurua indicated the rotting pile of bones.

"So, who exactly is, was, he? He seems like a he somehow."

"He is, was for many years, the Librarian. He oversaw the construction of the library in this place and the relocation of the modern Coven archive from its old home. He passed away back in 1999, if I remember correctly. But dates have a limited meaning for me now, and he had already become an anti-social, mean-minded hermit, so no one noticed."

"Didn't he smell?" Holly wrinkled her nose at the thought.

"Probably. I was not in a condition to tell, but I sealed off the office. Not that anybody came down here. By the early '90s, he had stopped dealing directly with anyone below the position of Elder and, once he had passed, I intercepted all messages and responded on his behalf. It does not take much effort to say no. The Inner Coven did not exactly miss him, and his staff were simply grateful. Bureaucracy has both its own inertia and velocity. Things have been carrying on very satisfactorily without him for over a decade."

"And no one ever came down to check on him?"

"No."

"So, what did he die of, exactly? Did you kill him, by any chance? And if he was already dead, how did he agree to me undertaking cataloguing work in the Library?"

"It looked like a stroke, and I had no hand in it. As for you, I wanted you to come down here into the deep library. So, on this one occasion, I said yes on his behalf."

Holly sensed the truth in these statements but did not feel comfortable with Saurua's involvement in her return to the library.

"We'll come back to that later. Right now, I'd like to focus on the who, how, and why of you. Grindlebones, no!" The last statement was yelled in the direction of the marmalade cat who had used the interlude of human conversation to emerge from his corner and sniff his way around the pile of bones and dry meat at the desk. He was now attempting to gnaw off a digit from the right hand of the corpse. Reluctantly, he let go of his tasty prize, sidled over to Holly, and squeezed under her chair where he crouched down to await further developments, which he sensed were not far away.

"Sorry," said Holly, "that's cats for you. You were about to explain yourself. In detail."

The female figure nodded in acknowledgement and began, "I was Sister Victoria Gita Saurua, a witch of mixed parentage. My father was a British official in India and a mundane. My mother was Indian and a witch. I spent my early years in India, but most of my adulthood in the grey dampness of England. In January 1917, for reasons that to this day I do not understand, I was accused of espionage for the Imperial German Coven. I was innocent. I can only repeat that I do not know why I was accused. Maybe it was the colour of my skin? Maybe it was because I was a woman?

"The Grand Coven of Great Britain and its many dominions subjected me to the humiliation of a Clerihorn to get at the truth. The ritual was conducted in the underground hall used by the Coven at that time for interrogation purposes. In those days, it was concealed beneath the iron and steam of St. Pancras Station sidings. Now it contains the Coven's consolidated library and is buried beneath its modern archives and the mundane library above. This office is on the furthest edge of the old hall and forms a connection between the library, as it now is, and The Grand Coven's grand new hall beneath the St Pancras Station hotel.

"My Clerihorn was a debacle from start to finish. The Coven had found me guilty before it even commenced. They produced a weak-minded and immature witch, barely in command of his own powers, to take the part of the Clerihorn and channel my witchlight. He did not have the strength to do things properly and crumpled under the strain. Everything collapsed and imploded. I had been imprisoned in a medieval torture implement. My body was..." Sister Saurua paused and Holly sensed a wave of fierce, ragged emotion beginning to swell out from her, but it was restrained and pulled back at the last moment.

"My body was pierced, ripped, and damaged beyond repair, and what little of me was left inside the carcass was crippled mentally — trapped but unable to escape. My witchlight, however, had been released into the air by the cretin of a Clerihorn. Part of me was propelled outwards with my witchlight only to be embedded in the pit that enclosed us, caught in the leaked magic that was integral to it like a fly in a web. For ninety-three years, I existed as a tortured entity torn in two: part of me imprisoned in a rotting meat cage and the other half free to watch myself suffer whilst being chained to the physical location that held me. I leave it to you to imagine what that felt like."

The final sentence was delivered with a dry turn of phrase that made Holly think she might have got on well with Victoria Saurua under different circumstances. At the moment, however, she still did not trust her, but given the horrors she had just heard summarised, Holly felt the need to say something,

"I read the contemporary accounts of your Clerihorn. It was brutal. I'm sorry."

"There is no need to apologise. You were not responsible. You are my salvation."

"Come again?"

"I assume that expression is requesting a further explanation?" Saurua barely paused before continuing, "A split and tortured existence is not life. I wished to die, but the Coven would not release me from the prison of my corrupted flesh and was unable to release me from the magical web of this place. Why it chose to deny me that first blessing, I do not know. You would need to ask the Elders of the Inner Coven. As for the second freedom I sought, for all its grand posturing, the Coven had neither the knowledge nor the power to free me."

"So?"

"So, I was doubly a prisoner, and I suffered commensurately. The living corpse I had become was capable of nothing but pain. But this consciousness, welded to the escaped flow of my witchlight, could at least think. For a long time, that was all it could do. Then I learned to harness the residual power around me to listen, then learn, and finally read the books that came to surround me. I created this body of light for myself, so that, when I chose, others might at least know there was someone here." Saurua gestured to her pale, stained image. "I learned enough to know that certain things might be possible given enough power and the possibilities of Old Magic. I also learned that considerable power was already being accumulated by one old family: yours. I carried on listening and focused my attentions. It's easy when people don't know you are there. I came across the prophecies. They gave me further hope when hope was all I had.

"Then, without warning, you and Sister Ninanna Beldam crashed into my prison. So much power carelessly splashed about, ripping holes into the deeper parts of the library, soaking into the fabric of its structure and the soil and rock surrounding it. And then you murdered your grandmother and came into your full power, right here in this very library. So great a magical strength and with raw power to spare. What you wasted, I absorbed. It helped me grow stronger. Much stronger."

"It was self-defence, not mu..." Holly tried to interrupt, but Victoria Saurua was determined to have her say.

"Time passed. You returned. Things developed. I shaped the idea of another Clerihorn in those susceptible to its allure. When it came to the actual ritual, I used your Old Magic as it flowed through me to end my physical suffering. This seemed fair exchange for clearing your name. I hoped to share more of your witchlight, back there amongst the books, but instead it brought you to me. It doesn't matter. Your power, whoever wields it, can free me from this echo, as it did from my rotting carcass. It is time for me to go home, and you are going to help me do it. You are going to save me."

Sister Saurua paused as if waiting from an affirmation from Holly, but Holly's mind was racing around trying to work out how to unravel the knotted story she had been presented with.

Finally, Holly said, "I'm still confused. Will you help me understand your situation better? From what I know of the grim history of this place, other people — other witches — have suffered and died down here. What turned you into a living ghost and not them? Or are they here too? How is it you have become chained to the library when the full library, as it is now, wasn't here back in 1917?"

"I have told you what I know. My Clerihorn was botched, a travesty. Perhaps it was the sheer power of the implosion that created this shadow of me? I have read of the atomic explosions that came later. Weren't the outlines of the fallen burned into the very ground?"

Holly had a sudden painful vision of Partridge's carbonised outline where he had fallen on the library pentagram, trying to defend her from her grandmother. Both Partridge and Ninanna had died in the library that day.

"The implosion of my witchlight burned an echo of me into everything that surrounded the remains of my physical form. And no, it wasn't the full-sized archive and library it is now, but it was a Grand Coven meeting hall, prison, interrogation chamber, and repository. Many old books were held there, also many people. More than enough raw witchlight and tortured emotion had penetrated its walls, floor, and ceiling over centuries to prepare a receptive canvas of residual magic that was ready and able to capture my imprint. Something like primed magnetic tape, if that is a sufficiently modern analogy for you? The gathering and installation of the Coven's document hoard in one concentrated location merely introduced yet more residual magic to the equation, like varnish to a painted picture. I was further trapped within it, but it also brought additional magics I learned to draw upon. If the Coven had interrogated and tortured me elsewhere, maybe things would not have turned out as they did. But luck, or misfortune, as well as the Coven, brought me here."

Holly considered things further. "So, if that was you I saw in the library earlier today, and you've all but said it was, what exactly were you hoping to gain from drawing my witchlight away from me?"

"It was me, and I have already indicated that I need your power to end this half life. I simply tried to take some. You have more than enough to spare. A witch of your heritage and a practitioner of Old Magic can always draw down more."

Whilst this was true, Holly still felt exceedingly uncomfortable at the thought of someone trying to siphon off her power without even a by-your-leave. Basically, it was theft and a very personal form of theft to boot. Also, whilst Saurua hadn't ducked any of her questions, her answers hadn't always seemed especially forthcoming. There was always more to add when Holly questioned further.

"All right, you've mentioned prophecies and you've mentioned my grandmother. What do you really know about either — both? And whatever it is you know; how do you know it?"

"As I have stated, I have had years to familiarise myself with the contents of the library. I have studied it. When I came across the book of prophecies that you have subsequently found, I realised that others had considered it before me and taken it seriously enough to leave their marks and annotations. It offered me the hope of vague possibilities, but vague was not good enough. I needed to know more. On one occasion, Sister Ninanna Beldam visited the library. She sought the book out. I studied her and, when she left, made her the object of my research. She was a witch with a very long and distinctive history. It left trails, including those I was uniquely able to detect.

"When the pair of you brought your struggles to the library, I observed and listened and learned enough to convince myself that she had, indeed, been harvesting the power of your family line. Whichever one of you bested the other would almost certainly have the power I needed to end this purgatory. It turned out it was you.

"Eventually, you returned victorious to repair the library, and I believed I had found the one who would 'wield mighty power over everything that liveth and breatheth and over those that have formerly done so.' As one that has 'formerly done so,' I needed to know more about you."

"And?"

"And?"

"Come on. You know more than that. You appear to know the way Ninanna physically trapped the witchlight of the dead, or at least the almost dead. How did you learn that? And what about the Polaroid of me that was in the book of prophecy? Brother James must have stolen the photo, but how and why did it end up here, in the library, in a book that wasn't even revealed by my Old Magic search last year?"

"Sister Ninanna Beldam's methodology for capturing witchlight was alluded to in the marginalia of the book. I simply deduced the details of the process."

Holly was not convinced by this, but let it ride.

"And the photo? What about that?"

"Once I had seen and identified you, I needed to know more about you, but your history was mundane, and your trail was minimal. There was little information in the Coven archives, and I couldn't search elsewhere: This echo is trapped within its echo chamber. My physical form was useless and had neither the wit nor the physical ability to find you. I needed a go-between, as it were. You met Brother William James in person, I believe?"

"He was yours?"

"I did not presume to own him, but he was a susceptible lover of books who spent many, many hours in this library. I found I could influence him, persuade him, and eventually instruct him to do things. Before the disaster of my Clerihorn, I had been good at influencing and 'borrowing' animals. Some of that ability apparently lingered."

"So, you made him visit me?"

"Not exactly. I influenced his thinking. He was a Coven official. The Coven was interested in you, worried even. I nudged his thoughts so that he carried out Coven work in a manner that benefitted my cause. I needed to know more about you. He became my ears and eyes."

"Did you kill him?"

"No. Not directly, but I share some responsibility with your familiar." Saurua pointed straight at Grindlebones, who was still crouched under Holly's chair, watching her body of light with unblinking eyes.

"You need to explain that one."

"As a living witch with an affinity for animals, I could borrow their small furry bodies for brief periods of time. Whilst my current magics are not witchlight in the normal sense — except for that which I borrowed from you — I found it easier to influence Brother James if he transformed himself into an animal. Once transformed, I could borrow his body for up to ten minutes to escape this underground confinement. He liked rabbits. The sheer sweet joy of grass and sky after so many years underground cannot be underestimated.

"After his last visit to you, he remained very distracted, and it was easy to get him to transform himself into a rabbit again. As I sought to borrow his mind, we both lost focus just long enough for a fox to find him and seize his vulnerable carcass. The fox, however, was so absorbed in its prey that it did not notice a large ginger cat creep up beside him. The cat, or the fox, or both were eventually going to fulfil the demands of nature and kill the rabbit. I left the body to its demise."

"And Brother James?"

"Remained with his soon-to-be-rabbit corpse, until he did not."

This was said too matter-of-factly for Holly's comfort,

"You mean that you left him to die?"

"He was, to use a modern idiom I have read, 'collateral damage'."

"And that was okay with you, was it?"

"It was what it was. In nature, everything is always hungry, and life is routinely consumed."

"But you made him turn into a rabbit. If it hadn't been for you, he wouldn't have been on the food chain as a main course."

"I encouraged him to transform. I did not have the power to make him. As for his death, well, we all die. In that, Brother James was lucky. I wanted what Brother James had. I want what others have and the ability I once had. I want to die."

Holly found herself pitying the shade of a human in front of her, but she was also increasingly disquieted by where the conversation was headed and the tone of much of it. Confirmation that Grindlebones had had a paw in the execution of Brother James also made her uncomfortable, however perfectly natural it was for the cat. Her main disquiet was still reserved for Sister Saurua, however.

"Has there been any other collateral damage along the way?"

"No one else has died that I know of."

"But you have influenced others to do things you wanted them to do?"

"Prodded, nudged them to do what they wanted to do. I needed to get you here, to where I was and to where I am."

"So, Elders Nightingale and Cavendish were controlled by you?"

"Not controlled. I encouraged them to indulge their inherent desires. Given the proximity of this place to the Grand Hall of the Coven, I found I had some ability to mould one or two of the less inhibited Elders. I had less influence over them than with Brother James — they did not spend an inordinate time down here in the library — but I could cajole them."

"But by 'cajoling' them you created the climate for holding a new Clerihorn, and that could have killed me. It could have killed my partner Jake!"

"I did not believe that a witch as powerful as you would ever truly be at risk."

"And Jake?"

"He survived."

"But he could just as easily have not."

Saurua shrugged. Under the chair, Grindlebones responded to Holly's growing anger by expanding his fur into a ball of feline fighting spikes.

"What the Coven did to you was wrong, but it does not entitle you to adopt a cavalier disregard of others. Have you no empathy left? Where's the humanity your physical self pleaded for? You've used people without any regard to the implications. I know it's really minor in comparison to the other things you have done, but I assume it was you who tricked me with that image of Partridge Mayflower.

Playing on my still raw emotions would be a doddle for someone who doesn't give a shit about others."

"That was a thing I did not do."

Holly did not believe Saurua but could not see the point of challenging her further. Instead she took a deep breath and merely said, "But you seem to be behind virtually everything else that has been going on recently. To what end, Victoria? What have you gained? What is the purpose of all this manipulation and deceit?"

"I have already said, have I not, Sister Beldam? I want you to kill me."

CHAPTER 28

"And why, exactly, Sister Saurua, would I want to do that?"

"Because you naturally have the empathy you accuse me of lacking. Because you hate suffering. Because you do not wish me to suffer further. Because yours is the humanity. Because you…"

Holly sensed a fluttering around her thoughts and realised someone was trying to influence them magically. That someone could only be Victoria Saurua. Holly flicked away the fluttering with a surprisingly gentle but very focused waft of witchlight.

"Any empathy or concern I have is going to evaporate very rapidly if you try to manipulate me like that."

Saurua performed another of her increasingly annoying shrugs.

"As you wish. In my position, you, like me, would try anything you could to gain your freedom."

"Maybe, but that doesn't really answer my question. Why would I want to kill you? I am not a murderer."

"You have killed before, and I need your help. I cannot go free without it. You cannot go free. If I remain here like this, you will always be looking over your shoulder. I have proved I have enough power to limit and constrain you. Like that time when you first came to the Coven's Grand Hall, remember? And even though I may not always be able to reach you directly, I have proved I can manipulate others. While I exist in this state, you will always wonder, always doubt. Kill me and the doubt is over."

"Is that a threat?"

"No. It is a statement of fact."

Holly could see the cold truth of what Saurua said, but nevertheless felt the implied threat. She remained on her guard.

"I still don't fully understand why you can't end things yourself, if you want death so very much. What is it you are expecting me to do that you can't? You tried to steal my witchlight. Can't I just lend you the power to do what you need?"

"This echo of me is trapped within the raw magic and fabric of the original space the library now occupies, and then within the library itself. The Old Magic you released and have continued to release is a final sealant. I need you to remove the Old Magic you introduced to this place and release everything trapped beneath it, including me."

"And what happens to the layers underneath that you say you are also trapped in?"

"There is a way to release it all. Enter the library portal from the lower library, a thing I cannot do, and use Old Magic simultaneously to transport and to reverse the flow of the portal. Instead of transporting one person away from the lower levels of the library, it will transport the library away from itself."

"Which, though she hasn't mentioned it, will cause the library to explode, destroying it and everything in it, including you, Holly girl. It will also leave a very large hole in the Euston Road, disrupt London traffic for days, and destroy the entire British Library, causing multiple mundane human fatalities. All of which might be considered a bit extreme."

Partridge Mayflower, dressed in a grey shirt and dark-grey denim jeans was now standing in the defunct Chief Librarian's office directly behind Victoria Saurua. Neither Holly nor Saurua had noticed him come in. Holly's emotional control gave up the ghost, and the rustling in her head grew as frenzied as subdued rustling could. Beneath her chair there was further rustling, scrabbling, and a small, pitiful meow.

"Partridge?" Holly squeaked. She had intended a resounding exclamation, but her emotions got the better of her vocal cords.

"Yes and no. I'm merely an echo of who I was. An imprint of myself that I left behind in the library."

"So, who is the you who is in my head?'

"Don't know about that. You'd have to ask him, assuming you can. But imagine two photographic plates capturing the same flash of light, or two digital cameras photographing the same object from slightly different angles. The event is over and done, but the images remain. Both of them."

"So, you're telling me you're nothing more than a video?"

Sister Saurua interjected,

"No. He is like me. A true vestige. A remaining trace of what was, but a genuine conscious trace, whom I did not invite here." The last sentence was delivered with a strong note of disapproval.

"Did you not? But here I am anyway. I rather thought young Holly, here, needed to know the implications of what you were proposing. I can't imagine that you were going to tell her."

"And, of course, she couldn't work it out for herself because she is just a woman," Saurua hissed back.

"She is Holly and, I discovered, can do most things she puts her mind to. She just doesn't always put her mind to things as quickly as she should. Quite emotional and easily distracted, but that's because she is Holly, not because she is a woman."

"Excuse me, I'm still here, you know?" Holly interrupted.

The two deceased but apparently not-quite-dead witches interrupted their exchange and turned to look at her.

"You are my salvation. I have not forgotten you," came from Saurua.

"Ah yes, but a salvation, it appears, who is going to kill herself and blow up a large part of London, plus many innocent people along with it." This from Partridge.

"The Coven caused all this. Their deaths do not matter. They deserve them. They should consider themselves lucky."

"And the innocent, non-illuminated people going about their daily business up above us? And me?" Holly retorted. "What about us — or are we mere collateral damage?"

There was a pause, and then Sister Saurua simply replied, "I have suffered enough. It must end."

It was Partridge who responded. "You have suffered. We all have, and you have suffered more than many, but killing hundreds to free yourself is not an acceptable way to end this. You know there is another way. Why haven't you told Holly about that?"

"It is not reliable. Not guaranteed."

"And the grand explosive gesture is? Neither method has been tried before, and nothing in this life, or death, is guaranteed. I would prefer to find my peace knowing I had caused the minimum amount of suffering to others."

"Ahem, excuse me again," Holly interrupted. "I really am still here, you know. How about having a three-way conversation? What other method are we talking about?"

"It is part of his 'modern' knowledge. Let him tell you."

If Holly didn't know better, she would have said that Victoria Saurua was somehow jealous of Partridge's knowledge, or perhaps it was the fact that he had lived freely and long enough in the modern world to gain it.

Partridge smoothed back his hair in a way Holly was so familiar with, despite the fact that a body of light needed no such attention, and began, "When the portal was constructed, I was told — rightly or wrongly — that if someone or something living and carrying a sufficient amount of raw magic crossed from inside the portal into the darkness that surrounds it, they could cause an implosion that will draw out all nearby magics, including the trapped and latent magic that has built up in the library. This will almost certainly cause havoc with the non-standard dimensions of the library itself, its ability to expand and simply absorb new book stock, for example, but it will not damage the fundamental physical structure. Think of it as a magical poultice for drawing off excess magic. The drawback is that the living thing that crosses through the portal wall will also be sucked out into the oblivion of the universe."

"You mean killed?" Holly wanted to get that part totally clear from the start.

Partridge looked down at his feet, "Yes, they will die."

"So, to summarise, to save the two of you, I either have to die and take a chunk of London with me, or I can bugger up the library for a bit and still die?"

Sister Saurua's "Yes" seemed unduly quick and enthusiastic to Holly's ear.

Partridge was more hesitant. "There are several other things you should probably be aware of. It's not just us down here. Other living echoes have been created over the years. We are simply the strongest. I am the most recent, and Saurua's imprint was the most traumatic and witchlight laden. But there are other shadows who will also be set free. You would not be doing it just for us. Also, the books have their own consciousness, I believe. That may be what you are hearing in your head. It would also be released, along with my twin echo, if you think there is an impression of me within the consciousness. I do not know what the books would think of such an action. You would have to ask them.

"Finally, the living thing that crosses through the portal does not have to be you. Anything fully alive and carrying the right amount of wild magic would trigger the implosion. A familiar, say, temporarily gifted sufficient wild magic, could do it."

Partridge pointedly looked down, and Holly saw Grindlebones, who had surreptitiously extracted himself from under her chair, sitting at Partridge's feet and gazing up at him. Partridge automatically bent down to scratch the cat's ears, then straightened up again when he remembered that, in his incorporeal state, he couldn't.

Holly snapped, "You'd have me kill Grindlebones? The pair of you were virtually inseparable when you were... alive. He pined for months after you were killed. Is that how you reward his love and loyalty? Are you even who you claim to be or is this all just a further ghastly — or should I say ghostly — hoax?"

Partridge looked sombre. "I am all that is left of me and no, I do not want you to kill Grindlebones, but life following the loss of a witch or a familiar is difficult for the one left behind. If Grindlebones chooses to follow me into oblivion, that is his decision."

"As if a cat could knowingly make such a decision."

"Well, actually, I don't know about Barny, he's still a young and inexperienced familiar, but Grindlebones is able to make such a decision. Aren't you old boy?"

As if in confirmation, Grindlebones produced a small but positive sounding yeow and attempted to rub himself against Partridge's legs but was frustrated by Partridge's lack of solidity.

Holly was not giving in that easily. "So you are trying to persuade me that Grindlebones is willing to die so that you and he can pass over together to a land of milk, honey, and cat biscuits — or are you planning on entering the big pearly gates of Heaven side by side?"

"No, I am not telling you that, Sister Holly Beldam. What I am saying is that I want peace, an end to this half-life existence. I have no idea what comes after, but oblivion seems a better option than this, and I am relatively new to this condition. It's not been quite a year and a half since most of me died. I hate to think how I'd feel if I had to stay here for as long as Sister Saurua has. It has got to severely trouble the mind, or at least the consciousness." Partridge gestured loosely and circumspectly in Saurua's direction to suggest that her mental stability was in question. "You'll have to ask the book me — if he exists — what he thinks about it. Likewise Grindlebones, but if he feels my loss as much as I miss his presence, oblivion may be an attractive option. Many familiars lie down and die when their witch passes on. It is to your credit that he did not, but he has a right to choose."

Grindlebones yeowed again.

"But he's just a cat," Holly flared back.

"There you go again — so much feral magic inside you that you repeatedly overlook the blessing of a familiar. Yes, he's a cat, but he was *my* cat and more importantly, he was my familiar. Strong bonds develop over time. We had been together, kitten and boy, man and cat, for eighty-seven years."

"Eighty-seven years? I never knew…"

"You've still got a lot to learn, Holly Beldam, for all your undoubted power. You've not done badly for a largely self-taught witch, though you had a damn fine mentor, even if I say so myself, but there is always more to learn. Books can teach you many things. Have you consulted yours recently?"

Holly took this as a hint and tried to call up the internal dry rustling she had involuntarily grown used to this last year. She braced herself for the unreality shock of hearing Partridge's voice from another source, but it was the dry, impersonal bookish tones that spoke to her,

"We have been listening since you allowed us to. Based on what we know, both... existences in this room with you have spoken the truth. There are two possible ways to cleanse the library. Both are untried but could theoretically work. Only one option will cause minimum disruption to the library."

"And...?"

"...and?" the dry voice queried unemotionally.

"If they are right, as you say, both ways will destroy your consciousness. How do you... how does your Partridge Mayflower feel about this?"

Then it was Partridge's voice that answered her, though as far as Holly was concerned, there was a Partridge standing in front of her. It was all very perturbing.

"We have said before, I am no more than an echo of an echo, and I am not truly individual. Just a drop in an ocean, so to speak. A part of a broad sea of learning and knowledge that has developed down here. We are not alive. We will not miss existence, as you term it. The knowledge we carry may be missed, but much of it is already inside of you, so that part of us will continue, regardless."

"You'll stay inside my head?" Holly had seriously mixed feelings about this.

"Our knowledge will, but you will no longer have access to this contemporaneous conversation." The voice gradually returned to its natural dry tone. "We are not alive. We will not miss what we have never had. Peace or oblivion are both untried experiences and are therefore of interest to us."

"But if you don't exist, you will no longer experience anything."

"That in itself will be new. Or maybe it will be a return to what was. We will find out, or we won't."

Holly had no answer to that. There was so very much to consider and weigh up, but given the visible signs of agitation being displayed by Victoria Saurua, Holly was getting the sensation that the dead witch was not expecting to give her that much more thinking time.

Then again, how much more time did she actually require? Somehow, she had to assess Grindlebones' needs to her own satisfaction. The only other people with a direct view would be the Coven, and given everything, she was not really sure they deserved a say.

"Grindlebones," Holly crouched down and called the big ginger tom cat over. Visibly reluctant, and with repeated glances over his shoulder back at Partridge, Grindlebones padded over to Holly. "So, what do you think, sweetie? Partridge says you'd like to join him, but it would mean dying. Do you understand? Is that what you want?" Holly didn't find it at all unusual that she was scratching the ears of a marmalade cat while having a human conversation with him about life and death. Judging from the sneer on Victoria Saurua's face, she was clearly less accommodating of this uncommon human and feline interaction.

Grindlebones seemed happy to have his ears scratched, but he continued to glance over at his dead witch in a way that potentially gave Holly her answer. Nevertheless, she tried again verbally,

"You really do want to be with Partridge, don't you?"

Holly was rewarded with a plaintive meow.

Holly was slowly and uncomfortably working towards a conclusion she didn't totally like. Before she was obliged to accept that she had arrived there, however, there were other matters to be resolved. Holly turned her gaze back to Saurua, "These other vestiges you say are trapped down here with you. Who are they? How do they feel about this possible purge and why haven't I come across any of them?"

"What do they matter?" Victoria Saurua answered. Holly glared at her pointedly. "But if you must know of them, listen. Boost your hearing and simply listen."

Holly stood up with some trepidation and used her Old Magic to sharpen her hearing. She listened, more than a little fearful of what — or rather who — she might hear. She could hear her own breathing and the shallower breaths of Grindlebones echoing through the musty office. She could hear the rustling of a cockroach in one corner of the room, and then she heard sighs and whispers that grew in volume, but never louder than the footfalls of the cockroach. *"Rest. Peace. Sleep. No more. Free me. Free us. Help us."*

Holly hadn't expected so many voices. If she focused and thought about it, she could even tell who some of them were. There was the Head Librarian himself, who had died on the job, an elderly witch who had had a heart attack whilst browsing some illicit erotica, the small child who had been crushed by falling bookshelves (so much for health and safety), and the many, many anguished whispers of those who had been tortured and died at the hands of the Coven in the dark days before nothing but the library filled the entire subterranean space. The past had not been a pleasant place.

The one voice Holly had been preparing herself to hear, was not, however audible. Ninanna Beldam had died within the library's portal, shortly after killing Partridge, but her voice was not present. Holly had to ask, "Where's my grandmother? She's not here, but she died here. Why can't I hear her?"

Partridge looked thoughtful. "In the ways of Old Magic, you know far more than we do, Holly. I've told you that before, I recall. But, based on what I know for certain, she's not here. Based on what you've told me in the past about her powers, if her witchlight was anchored to something physical," Partridge glanced discreetly at the ornate moonstone ring on Holly's left hand, "any vestigial consciousness would stay with it. Assuming there was any vestigial consciousness in the first place, of course and, personally, and knowing what I know of your grandmother, I wouldn't be too quick to attempt to check if there was. Sleeping dogs should remain sleeping in my book, eh, Holly girl?"

Holly found herself reassured by Partridge's words, but somehow, she needed something more before committing herself. She turned back to Grindlebones who was still hunkered down at her feet.

"Grindy? Grindlebones? Show me what you want."

Grindlebones mewed loudly and decisively and padded purposely over to Partridge, sat down, and purred so loudly that Holly did not need her enhanced hearing to get the full benefit.

"There, you have your answer. The cat is more decisive than you are." This from Sister Saurua. "There is no need for any further prevarication. I demand that you free me. Now."

Without warning, a wall of fierce and tangible emotion smashed into Holly. There was misery, pain, loneliness, and rage, but mostly it was undiluted rage, raw and throbbing. Holly felt as if she was drowning in Saurua's chaotic feelings. They engulfed her, spun her around and blotted out everything else. Unable to breathe, she lost all sense of time and direction. She could still see Saurua, abandoned within her own anger, and Partridge, who appeared to be oblivious to what was going on, but they were distant. It was as if she was trapped within a tank of deep churning water rather than the underground office of the former Librarian. Holly gasped and flailed helplessly, but it got her nowhere. Her lungs were already starting to hurt, and she realised that if she continued to thrash about and panic, she was going to be suffocated by the emotional tsunami Saurua had unleashed.

Holding her breath as best she could, Holly willed herself to relax and stay still. With the enforced calm came focus. Holly used her re-found focus to bring her own wild magic under control and to use it to absorb and subdue Saurua's frenzy.

Like a struggling swimmer, Holly found herself surfacing through the chaos. As she finally came up for air, the rage flowed away and dissipated. Saurua was standing in the office unmoving, to all intents and purposes, once again calm. Holly took a huge, much-needed breath and immediately swathed the woman in magical tranquillity. She was so lost in her own thoughts, she didn't appear to notice.

Holly glanced over at Partridge, who was still crouched down, talking to an ecstatic Grindlebones. But sensing Holly's gaze, he looked across at her,

"It's your decision to make: yours and Grindlebones. But once you've made it, I can help you with the technical side of things, like how much Old Magic needs to be carried through the portal wall. First, though Holly, you really do need to reach a decision."

CHAPTER 29

Holly had made her decision and was now sitting at the Head Librarian's desk, on the opposite side to its crumbling former owner. The desk had been thoroughly wiped clean of the detritus of times past and in front of her were the original construction plans for the library, which Partridge had directed her to.

"They'll help you with the technical side of purging the library. Though if you added any augmentations of your own when you sorted out the library last year, you'll have to resolve those yourself."

Given everything she had learned recently, Holly was wondering how efficacious her sorting out of the library had really been. The Old Magic she had used seemed to have complicated things rather amazingly. On the plus side, because of the information she had 'downloaded' from the library the previous year and now more recently, she at least found she could interpret the plans without any difficulty.

It appeared that if she draped Grindlebones in a relatively small but highly charged ball of her Old Magic infused witchlight, transported into the portal with him, and then at the right point pushed him into the moving starlit night that surrounded the portal column, she would have no more than forty-five seconds to get out of the portal and seal the top end of the column before everything imploded and sucked all the latent magic out of the library and its surroundings.

If she didn't manage to get out and complete all essential tasks within forty-five seconds, she would die — the unsealed implosion could blow up and out into the upper library and claim other lives.

Alternatively, if she left it too late to present Grindlebones to the surrounding night, the stars might have disappeared from the column and nothing would happen except she might inadvertently kill Grindlebones to no good end and damage the portal irrevocably, leaving her trapped within it indefinitely.

She calculated the right moment to let Grindlebones go would therefore be precisely thirty-five seconds before she arrived in the pentagram area in the upper library and before the final stage of transition kicked in. Having said that, all timings were subject to variation. Holly figured she had a margin of no more than ten seconds to play with.

Simple, really — not.

Holly looked up from the paperwork to find Partridge, Victoria Saurua, and Grindlebones all staring at her intently.

"It's doable, just. Maybe. I'll need to take some time to prepare the lower library for the damage that is likely to occur when its alternative dimensions are removed. I also want to time the ascent through the portal so that I know precisely when and where I need to do things. Finally, though I'm sure that at least two of you will think I'm overly sentimental, I need Grindlebones to convince me, one more time, that he really wants to do this."

Partridge unhesitatingly nodded his agreement. Victoria Saurua, however, scowled, and, for a brief moment, Holly sensed the earlier chaotic rage mixed with the same tangible, malevolent presence that had successfully held her down in her chair that first time in the Coven's Grand Hall. It most definitely wasn't pleasant. This time, knowing what she was experiencing, Holly could detect both strong malice and an all-powerful desire for vengeance, whatever the cost. There was an absence of... humanity. Or perhaps, if Holly was minded to be generous, the humanity was still there but had been drowned out by the more powerful negative feelings. At least, by having a greater understanding of it, Holly was prepared. A visible stream of bright white witchlight flowed from Holly and blocked the power emerging from around Saurua. The woman's scowl deepened further, and she tried to increase the power she wielded, but she could do nothing to deflect Holly.

"If you really want me to help you, I'd stop doing that, if I were you," Holly said loudly and clearly. Inwardly though, the witch's display of unchecked frustration and latent malevolent power had further convinced Holly that she really did need to cleanse the lower library before things got further out of hand.

Holly tentatively eased her magic from around the angry witch and, when nothing immediately happened, turned her back on her in order to commence her preparations. It was Grindlebones, his eyes firmly fixed on the still visibly seething apparition, who realised something was about to take place. He yowled loudly, just as another burst of dark controlling power was released by Sister Saurua. Holly whipped round, and in one flash of her own magic, surrounded Saurua in a more powerful dose of restraining magic. There was a brief, intense struggle, but, because of Grindlebones' advance warning, Holly's power was once again dominant.

Holly stood directly in front of Saurua.

"I don't know how I can make this any clearer, but all you are doing is losing my support and sympathy. And there is no need. I am going to finish things if I possibly can, but everything I do from here on in is for Partridge and Grindlebones and all the others trapped in the library, but mostly it is for Partridge. You have suffered abominably and unfairly, but it doesn't justify your actions now."

Leaving Saurua bound in white witchlight, something she really did not like doing given the woman's history of torture and incarceration, Holly went off down the corridor outside the office to the library to make her preparations.

Three trips up and back down the portal, and Holly had calibrated her timings as finely as she could manage. She then went to survey the book stacks and altered dimensions of the library. Her review complete, she came to the conclusion that, as she was about to purge the whole edifice, releasing more Old Magic into it in the short term was unlikely to cause any lasting harm. The final cataloguing of the library and its computerisation was therefore completed in only several minutes of concentrated witchlight flow.

During the process, the whole area was bathed in cold white fire so bright that Holly had to produce a pair of really dark glasses to protect her eyesight. Once it was over, Holly couldn't work out if it had been a good thing or a waste of time to have spent so long previously cataloguing the books using only minimal magics.

All the while Holly was making her preparations, Victoria Saurua remained in the Chief Librarian's office, bound in Holly's witchlight. Now was not a time to be taking chances, Holly realised, though she deeply regretted keeping an already traumatised long-term captive prisoner.

Her preparations finally complete, Holly returned to the office to find Grindlebones and Partridge companionably wrapped around one another, although technically Grindlebones was actually surrounded by the non-corporeal Partridge. The constrained fury of Victoria Saurua was still painfully visible. Holly felt both guilty and relieved about her restraining use of witchlight.

"I'm almost ready to do things," Holly addressed the room, "but, as I've already indicated, I still have major qualms about using Grindlebones in this activity. If the requirement is merely for something living to penetrate the portal, why don't I just drape the cockroach in the corner with witchlight and let him go?"

Partridge looked both lost and relieved at the same time. Grindlebones, however, meowed loudly and burrowed further into Partridge's lap, or rather Partridge himself, given his lack of solidity. Partridge looked down and into himself in a confused, but clearly delighted manner. Holly crouched down in front of Partridge and his familiar.

"What are you trying to tell me, Grindlebones?" The cat meowed even louder and hunkered down still further into Partridge. In the corner of the room, Victoria Saurua could be heard swearing colourfully and bitterly under her breath.

"Do you want to stay here with Partridge?" The cat's wide yellow eyes stared, unblinking, at Holly. "Do you want to free Partridge?" the yellow eyes blinked and Grindlebones meowed plaintively. "Do you understand that if you free him, you are going to die alongside him?" Another blink. Another meow. "And are you okay with that?" There was an infinitesimal pause and then Grindlebones blinked and meowed again.

"Okay, just a few more questions, old boy. Would you like a final feast of avocado and tomato?" Silence. The yellow eyes stared and did not blink. "Would you like a meal of salmon and custard?" Further silence and unblinkingness. "Would you like a meal of salmon in jelly, the really expensive brand?" Blink, blink, and many meows.

Holly shook her head in a well-I-never sort of way and pointed directly in front of Grindlebones. His favourite bright green plastic bowl appeared, filled with the expensive brand of salmon and jelly he was partial to. Grindlebones stuck his nose straight into the food and started eating noisily.

"And you are really, really sure you are prepared to die in order to release Partridge?"

The ginger head came up, two clear yellow eyes blinked rapidly, and there was a loud meow. Behind Holly, there was a triumphant shriek from Victoria Saurua followed by a stream of venomous profanity,

"You have had your bloody answer. Time and fucking time again. Why do you keep asking things? Why don't you just shut the fuck up instead? You have to take action now. Why do you keep buggering about over a fucking stupid cat when you happily slaughtered your own grandmother in cold blood?"

Holly took a deep breath and responded firmly, but surprisingly calmly, "Wherever did you learn such foul language? I'm sure it really wasn't ladylike to swear like that when you were truly alive. For your information, I am taking my bleeding time in order to let Grindlebones finish his meal and prepare himself. You will get what you want, but to do this, I am risking myself and killing Grindlebones, so things will be done in my way and in my own time. Please remember, for a little while longer, what it was like to be human and have a familiar — or at least love something other than yourself."

Saurua didn't respond. Grindlebones carried on eating and purring simultaneously. Being a cat, it didn't take him long to consume the entire bowlful.

Partridge looked at Holly. "Better get going, girlie, if you're going for it. The boy here seems ready."

Holly nodded slowly. "Are you ready? Are you sure you want this? We'll go to the portal to finalise things soon. Once I imbue Grindlebones with my witchlight, we won't have much time. We'll have to enter the portal immediately, and then everything will need to happen according to precise timings. If I get this wrong, they'll be two of the living passing over, not just one. Do you want to say goodbye to Grindlebones before we start?" From the back of the office there were further barrack room profanities from Saurua, but at least she was now once again swearing more or less under her breath.

Partridge replied gently, "No. The boy and I are good. We have an… understanding. All that needs to be known, is."

"What about us? I mean, we… we didn't really get to say goodbye last time, and now you are about to die all over again, and…"

"I know," Partridge said softly. We said what was needful and what we could. Sometimes, that's the best way. The rest… well, it was real, so I know what I need to. There's no need for tears. They'll only get in the way of your timings. Save 'em for later, if you need to cry, but Grindlebones and I both want this. Eighty-seven years together is a long time. You and yours will learn in due time. Provided you get your timings right, of course."

Partridge raised his eyebrows in a 'I'm telling you you'd better get them right' sort of way.

"Will you bleeding hearts bloody well get on with it?" Saurua was not going to make things easy. She was once again struggling vigorously against Holly's witchlight constraints.

Holly pulled herself together tightly. "Right, it's time. Partridge. Thank you. For everything. I've missed you. I'll miss you again, and the boy here. Both. Very, very much. I love you both."

Holly swallowed hard and looked down at Grindlebones. "Ready boy? Come on then."

Holly turned and walked decisively to the office door. She heard the click of cat paws and claws following her without hesitation. As she walked out of the door, she slackened the restraints around Saurua, ever so slightly, but not enough to free her. She hoped her "bleeding heart" humanity was not misplaced but thought there was little enough time left for Saurua to do any damage.

Holly was so intent on what was to come next, she didn't notice the puff of dust that began billowing across the floor behind her and Grindlebones. They continued towards the portal. So did the dust. Then it accelerated, a small wind dervish with a mission of its own.

At the bottom of the portal, Holly paused long enough to drape a bright skein of white witchlight around Grindlebones. The swirl of dust made a final effort to reach them, but just as it got there, Holly picked Grindlebones up in her arms and transported herself and him into the portal. Holly gently nuzzled his fur. Grindlebones purred deeply. They began to rise, and the seconds ticked away all too quickly. At precisely the right time — at least she hoped it was — she kissed Grindlebones on the nose and held him out towards the moving starlight of the portal sides.

With a single meow, Grindlebones stepped forward and through the moving wall. He disappeared immediately.

Holly swallowed hard, but kept her eyes fixed on the expensive and extremely accurate watch she had acquired for the process.

The seconds now dragged on with an unexpected slowness, right up until the final five, which rushed past without even a goodbye.

Holly arrived alone in the pentagram area of the upper library. She stepped onto the ornate marquetry design of the pentagram without hesitation and sealed the portal entrance with a flash of blinding white witchlight. If she was aware of the extreme tightness of the timing, or if it reminded her of her final fraught confrontation with Ninanna, she didn't let it show.

A nano-second after the seal was complete, there was a muffled detonation deep below her, followed by the sound of a wild wind roaring past and away and away again until it was no more.

This, in turn, was followed by the repeated thuds of books and bookshelves falling over on top of one another. Someone was going to be faced with one hell of a clean-up job, thought Holly, just before the alarms in the upper library kicked in and pandemonium prepared itself to descend upon her.

Down in the lower library, the dust finally settled.

CHAPTER 30

Holly was sitting at her kitchen table at the Basingfield Lane house. Barny was curled up asleep on her lap. The pair of them had been joined at the hip for each of the thirty-six hours since Holly had returned home alone from the library. Barny had even accompanied Holly to her meeting with Elder Graham as she explained to her how and why the Coven's precious library had come to be a chaos of multiply stacked bookshelves and why, unbeknownst to it, the Coven had been needing a new Chief Librarian for some time.

Right at the moment, Holly was sipping her third cup in a row of steaming Lapsang Souchong and steadily working her way through a box of man-size tissues. The resultant balls of soggy paper were scattered on the floor around her feet. Barny was catfully resisting the urge to go and play with them, but then again, he really wasn't in the mood for play right now. His witch's nose was decidedly red, and her eyes were pink. For reasons Barny could not quite fathom, this made him think of rabbits. Even rabbits didn't make him feel any better. Life was far from carefree right now.

Holly had tried very hard not to give in to her grief, but she missed Partridge — was missing him all over again — and now the added loss of Grindlebones was cutting pretty deep. Barny was clearly feeling his loss too. Sensing her familiar's upset just made hers worse. The empty bright green cat bowl visible in the utility room didn't help, either.

And then, of course, there was Jake.

Barny sensed something was happening before Holly did. He meowed and leapt from her lap just as the phone rang. It was a voice message of sorts, but not one that had ever found its way along a traditional copper wire. The world of witchery liked to pay lip service to modern communications equipment, but it was just for show. You never found a witch carrying a mobile phone if they could help it. Holly, of course, was the exception. Past habits died hard.

As Holly went to pick up the phone, it loudly announced, "Elder Caprice Graham would welcome the opportunity to talk to Sister Holly Beldam at her earliest convenience."

"What now," sighed Holly out loud and in less-than-resigned tones. Barny said nothing but stood leaning against Holly's right leg in anticipation of another journey somewhere. Holly scooped him up in her arms, transported them both to the cottage in Oxfordshire, and then produced Caprice's calling card. Jake might not be around anymore, but Holly was still attempting to limit the Coven's access to her mundane home.

Holly focused on Caprice's card, and as soon as non-visual contact had made said, "Is now a good time to talk?"

"Sure, why not? I'll open up a portal for you, and you can come on over so we can chat in person."

"Give me one minute." Holly waved a hand in front of her face and quickly eradicated all signs of recent crying. She then took Barny and the card into the cottage's back garden. There was no way she wanted to open up a portal to the Inner Coven directly from her lounge, even if it was the officially magical one. After everything, she felt the need, more than ever, to be cautious in her dealings with the Coven.

The edges of the calling card began to glow deep red. Holly tossed it into the air where it hovered and expanded. Holly, with Barny in her arms, stepped up into it and disappeared.

An hour or so later, Holly, with Barny now at her heels, re-emerged from a large, crimson edged, rectangular portal in the garden. A second later, she caught a piece of plain white card as it fluttered down to earth. Barny and she then took the now well-trodden walk across the cottage's garden, through the orchard's trees, into the field at the back of the Basingfield house, over the garden fence, through the back garden, and into the house via the back door.

Once more seated at the kitchen table, Holly re-settled Barny on her lap, magicked up her fourth cup of Lapsang, and said, "Well, what do you make of that, Barny?"

"If you two have been off somewhere together, I'm guessing he already has an opinion. So, how about telling me what's up?"

"Jake!" Holly exclaimed. "What are you doing here? Come in. Sit down. Would you like a cup of tea?"

Holly allowed her voice to express her happy excitement, but somehow kept the physical urge to jump up and throw herself at full tilt into Jake's arms in check. She didn't yet know why he had come calling.

Jake companionably pulled up a kitchen chair.

"I've come to visit you. I took the liberty of letting myself in, but then I realised you weren't here. I was about to turn round and go out again when I heard you and Barny coming back across the garden. I thought I'd wait and surprise you. So 'Surprise!' I guess. I've brought you some flowers."

Jake produced a large bunch of red and yellow roses that he had managed to secrete somewhere unseen.

"Oh, they're lovely. Thank you so much. What's the occasion?"

"No particular occasion. Not yet, anyway," Jake smiled a little sheepishly. "Why don't you tell me what's up?"

"I've just been offered a job."

"Well that's brilliant. Congratulations. I didn't know you'd been applying."

"Neither did I. I mean, I hadn't, but, well, it's a long story. Basically there's one hell of a clean-up job required at the library and, on the grounds that I'm the one person who fully understands what's been going on and have the only complete record of all the library stock, the Coven has just offered me the position of Chief Librarian."

Jake hesitated slightly. "And, given your relationship with the Coven, you'd want to take it because…?"

"Actually, I haven't decided yet, but the main incentive would be that I'd automatically become an Elder of the Inner Coven and party to their thinking and decision-making. The Coven could do with a good shake up, and I'd be in a position to do some shaking, I think.

I would have an opportunity to make a difference and put some bad things right — or I could hate every moment of it. But either way, I could keep a close eye on what the other Elders are up to."

In addition, Holly sensed it would provide some structure and focus to her activities and present her with a not insignificant challenge to overcome. She responded to a good challenge. It would also mean she would actually be involved in the day-to-day world of witchery rather than sitting on the side-lines, as she had been doing for the last year or so. She recognised she could do with getting to know some more practising witches. She did not, however, explain any of this to Jake. Now did not seem to be the right time.

"Sounds to me like you've already made your mind up."

"No. Not really. There are some seriously major downsides too, the out-dated attitudes of most of the current Inner Coven included. Plus, I'd trust the whole lot of them as far as I could throw them, but maybe it's better to distrust them close-up, than from a blind-sided distance? Isn't there something about keeping your friends close, but your enemies closer? There's a lot been going on since you haven't been around. And then, well, there's you and us, possibly, and where we're at and how me having a role at the Coven might affect us, or not, depending…"

Holly looked questioningly at Jake. She couldn't help but feel that all the things that had recently happened — and that she badly wanted to tell him about — would only serve to alienate him further. If that was true, the job of Chief Librarian was likely to be the straw that caused irrevocable damage to the dromedary-like spine of their relationship. Holly so didn't want that, but, height aside, she didn't want to end up playing the role of the little woman. She had power and she needed to use it fully. If Jake didn't like that…

Jake looked uncomfortable and shifted awkwardly on his chair. "That's sort of what I called round to talk about, if that's okay with you?"

Holly automatically tensed in anticipation of what was to come. On her lap, Barny curled himself into a tighter ball, partially in witch/familiar solidarity and partially to avoid any excessive and soggy hugging that might shortly be headed in his direction.

"Okay," said Holly tentatively. Her 'okay' sounded more questioning than affirmative.

Nevertheless, Jake took it as permission to begin. "I've been doing a lot of thinking, Prickles. I know things with us haven't been good recently, and I realise that it was me who gave up and walked out, not you. It was stupid. I was stupid, really stupid. If I'm honest, the problem wasn't us as a couple. You see, I've been struggling to come to terms with your 'witchlight'. That's the correct way to refer to it, isn't it? I'm still uncertain, even about that. For me, it's all still new and frightening. The whole discovery of magic being real is frightening — not your magic especially, although that is a bit frightening too, to me, at least. So, I was uncomfortable and scared. The stuff with those guys from the Coven served to push me over the edge. But now, I have had time to think and reflect. I've been doing a lot of thinking, but I've told you that already, haven't I...?"

Holly nodded encouragingly and tried very hard not to squeeze Barny unduly.

Jake continued, "Since I walked out, the one thing that has been consistent and unrelenting is that I miss you: constantly, miserably, badly. I love you, and I have finally realised that the you I love includes your magic and witchlight and whatnot. It's part of you, but I figure that I've made it difficult for you to be you because you've been trying to compartmentalise things for my benefit and keep things that matter to you away from me because I can't deal with them and that's not good and damages you and us and...

"Oh, sod it, Holly. What I'm trying very badly to say is that I love you, still love you, haven't stopped loving you, despite my appalling behaviour. I'm miserable when I'm away from you, and I want to come back home, if you'll have me?"

Jake paused briefly and read the resultant silence as negative. He took a deep breath,

"I know things would have to change. I'm not ducking that. The job offer sounds good. Maybe mixing more with other witches would be good. You say that other couples have mixed magic/non-magic marriages? Perhaps we could learn from them, or there's support groups or something. I..."

Jake found he couldn't go on talking because he suddenly had his arms and lower face full of Holly and Barny and an inordinate amount of Barny's fur, as Barny had found himself transported with Holly from one side of the kitchen table to the other.

Holly used Jake's muffled silence as an opportunity to share her own highly excited thoughts. "Jake, I've missed you so much, sweetheart. I gave you the space you asked for. I've been scrupulous about it, but I've hoped and hoped you'd come back. I've tried so hard to respect your needs, because I love you and I know that magic can be daunting. I didn't want you thinking I was manipulating you, but I haven't, and it's been your decision and…and… just come back. Please."

At this point, various things happened almost simultaneously, or in such rapid succession that they might as well have been simultaneous. Holly started crying, largely from happiness, but also from the emotional aftermath of everything. Jake started crying because Holly was crying and also from relief and his share of the communal emotive happiness. Barny purred in response to everyone's happiness, but leapt for safety because, as much as he loved his witch, too many salt tears were bad for both a cat's fur coat and his dignity. Plus, he was in serious danger of being squashed between Holly and Jake, and he figured they would be needing private time any time soon.

Holly, ecstatic that Jake had come back to her without magical intervention, but recognising that magic nevertheless had its uses in the complicated ways of romance, transported herself and Jake — still in the time-honoured clinch of happy endings — upstairs to their waiting bed.

Downstairs in the utility room, Barny was sniffing hopefully at an empty bowl and wondering whether to go out in search of a fresh meal or simply open a can. He missed Grindlebones, and the old boy had taught him many interesting things before he went to be with his own witch. Opening a tin of cat food without a can opener was just one of them. Barny planned to show his witch more of them one day. Just not today. Judging from the happy sounds emanating from upstairs, it seemed she would be otherwise engaged for some time to come.

ABOUT THE AUTHOR

J.S. Watts is a British poet and novelist. Her work appears in a diversity of publications in Britain, Ireland, Canada, Australia, New Zealand, and the United States and has been broadcast on BBC and Independent Radio. She has edited various magazines and anthologies.

She has published six books to her name in addition to *Old Light*: poetry collections, *Cats and Other Myths* and *Years Ago You Coloured Me*, plus multi-award nominated SF poetry pamphlet *Songs of Steelyard Sue* and her most recent poetry pamphlet, *The Submerged Sea*. Her novels are *A Darker Moon* – dark literary fantasy and *Witchlight* – paranormal (published in the US and the UK by Vagabondage Press). See www.jswatts.co.uk for further details.

Witchlight

J.S. Watts

SEE HOW IT ALL STARTED

Witchlight

In this humorous urban fantasy, Holly has been mortal all her life. Now at thirty-eight, her fairy godfather arrives to tell her she's a witch, and suddenly she's having to come to terms with the uncertainties of an alarmingly magic-fuelled world. Magic is not like it is in the books and films, and Holly starts to doubt whether her fairy godfather, Partridge Mayflower, is the fey, avuncular charmer he appears.

As a new romance blooms, appearances become magically deceptive, and Holly can't afford to trust those closest to her, including herself. Accidents start to happen, people die, Old Magic is on the hunt, but in the age-old game of cat and mouse, just who is the feline and who is the rodent?

An unusual take on the fantasy chick lit genre, Witchlight is no ordinary paranormal romance, and Holly is no ordinary witch. J.S. Watt proves that wonder, magic -- and love -- wait around the corner at every stage in life. And just when we think we have it all figured out, fate sets us on another unexpected adventure and has us fighting to protect our own.

www.ingramcontent.com/pod-product-compliance
Lightning Source LLC
Chambersburg PA
CBHW020604250626
47154CB00004B/1350